Readers love
ANDREW GREY

Eastern Cowboy

"Grey does a great job of creating realistic, moving characters, and Tanner and Brighton are two of my favorites."
—Watch & Word Society

Stranded

"A great story of how time passes and people allow their relationship to settle into routine… This doesn't mean that they are no longer deeply in love, sometimes they just need a reminder."
—Gay List Book Reviews

"Stranded is an amazing combination between an intense thriller-like stalker story, a sizzling romance, and a character study which, through tension and drama, brings out the worst and the best in both main characters."
—Rainbow Book Reviews

A Daring Ride

"All the things we've come to love from Grey are there in the print. An emotional, engrossing, and sexy ride is what's in store with this latest work from one of the best authors in the genre."
—MM Good Book Reviews

"Sweet and sexy rodeo romance with a focus on the challenges of coming out to a non-supportive family."
—The Romance Reviews

Readers love
ANDREW GREY (cont.)

Love Comes Unheard

"I really enjoyed this installment and highly recommend it and the series."

—The Blogger Girls

"I have come to enjoy these books and always look forward to the next one."

—Scattered Thoughts and Rogue Words

The Gift

"Mr. Grey has given us a wonderful story of love and hope and I hope you each grab a copy and enjoy."

—House of Millar

Spirit Without Borders

"Nobody writes like Andrew Grey. I pick up one of his books and start reading, and I can't put it down. This one definitely was one of those books."

—Inked Rainbow Reviews

"The realistic picture Andrew paints about the conditions, the area, the lives of these people grips you and you become emotionally involved in the story and you won't want to put it down until you finish."

—Ranbow Gold Reviews

By ANDREW GREY

Published by DREAMSPINNER PRESS
www.dreamspinnerpress.com

Published by DREAMSPINNER PRESS
www.dreamspinnerpress.com

EYES
ONLY ME
FOR

ANDREW GREY

DREAMSPINNER PRESS

Published by
DREAMSPINNER PRESS

5032 Capital Circle SW, Suite 2, PMB# 279, Tallahassee, FL 32305-7886 USA
www.dreamspinnerpress.com

Eyes Only for Me
© 2015 Andrew Grey.

Cover Art
© 2015 L.C. Chase.
http://www.lcchase.com
Cover content is for illustrative purposes only and any person depicted on the cover is a model.

ISBN: 978-1-63476-686-9
Digital ISBN: 978-1-63476-687-6
Library of Congress Control Number: 2015911624
First Edition November 2015

Printed in the United States of America
∞
This paper meets the requirements of
ANSI/NISO Z39.48-1992 (Permanence of Paper).

To Dominic, for everything you do for me.

CHAPTER 1

I PARKED my car away from the house in order to give the other guests room to park. I popped the trunk, then lifted out my large cooler bag. The street was quiet—too quiet. I walked up to Ronnie's place, past the garage doors, which were closed, and to the back door. I set down the cooler and pulled out my phone. Yeah, I had the right day, and the text to prove it:

Where are you, Buttmuncher? Don't forget the party today.

That had been sent two hours ago, in typical Ronnie style. I had finished what I was doing and said I'd be there an hour before the party started. Of course I would be there early; the man had no sense of style at all. Every summer he had one of these parties. They started at four and ran until whenever. Actually, they usually ran until everyone came to the realization that they'd had way too much booze and that there wasn't going to be any real food available. Then they'd start to leave in search of something to eat to keep from chewing their own arms off.

I looked through the windows beside the door and saw nothing. I knocked, then tried the door. It was open, so I went inside. "Ronnie," I called. "I'm here." I grabbed the cooler and hauled it inside, closing the door behind me. The house was quiet, eerily so, especially when there would be forty people there within an hour. "Wherever you are, I'm going to put the stuff I brought in the fridge." I went into the spotless kitchen. Everything gleamed: the counters, the stove, the sink. Of course they did, because they were never used. Ronnie never cooked. I was surprised the stainless-steel cooktop didn't still have the protective plastic covering. It was that clean.

"Jesus Christ," I muttered to myself when I opened the refrigerator door. Protein drinks, Red Bull, two cans of Diet Coke

1

from the last time I was here, an old banana, which I threw out, and a tray of Jell-O shots. That was all. The beer for the party sat on the counter, still warm. With a sigh, I put the contents of the cooler bag in the fridge. "Ronnie, where the hell are you?"

I noticed the master bedroom door was closed, and I walked over to it, wondering if he'd fallen asleep or something. I heard rhythmic thumping from behind the door, then Ronnie's voice as he said, "Yeah, baby, that's it! Right there. You got it."

"Ronnie!" I called and banged sharply on the door. "Finish whatever you're doing, for God's sake. You asked me to get here early." I rolled my eyes. "If the party is a flop, it's your funeral."

I heard a squeak and a thump. Two seconds later the door flew open and a very naked Ronnie stepped out of the room, flushed, cock slick and pointed at the sky. I swallowed and tried not to look. Well, what I tried to do was look like I wasn't looking, but that was damn difficult. "I'm busy."

"Half your clients will be here in forty-five minutes," I warned, knowing it would not be good if his multimillion-dollar clients found their financial representative naked and still in bed with his girlfriend.

"Shit." He turned, and I couldn't resist a slap across his ass. Yeah, it was copping a feel, and I was ashamed the minute I did it, but fucking hell. The man had an ass to die for… and that went along with the rest of him: rich Mediterranean skin, a body that had been worked and toned for years at the gym, powerful legs, and wide shoulders.

"I'll get things ready for you. Just finish up and get out here," I told him. He waved and kicked the door closed, and I went back into the kitchen because the last thing I needed to hear was him having sex. I knew it was stupid, but I had a crush on the guy. First, he was straight. He was also my friend—my best friend—and I wasn't about to put that in jeopardy.

I went into the dining room and found exactly what I expected to see: the table was covered with various packages of cookies, chocolate, pretzels, chips, and for dessert… gummy bears. My teeth ached almost instantly. "For God's sake, Ronnie, you're almost forty years old, and you aren't living in a frat house any longer." I rearranged the sugar buffet on the table along the side, then went into the kitchen and got bowls for the chips and pretzels. As I was looking, I found hot dog and hamburger buns in a cupboard. "Again, these are clients, not frat brothers."

Ronnie came out of the bedroom, dressed this time.

"You have clients coming to the party, right?"

He nodded.

"Top clients who trust you with millions of dollars, right?"

"Your point?" Ronnie asked in a huff.

"Do you still want them as clients tomorrow?" I asked him seriously.

"Of course I do." He put his hands on his hips in a typical Ronnie passive-aggressive move.

I shook my head and held out my hand.

"What's that for?" he asked.

"Money. If you want me to save your ass and keep everyone from talking about your dud party, give me money now." Ronnie snatched his wallet off the counter and handed me a couple of twenties. I snatched the wallet and grabbed all the cash. "Saving your ass. Not a frat party." I stepped closer. "Remember when your assistant Joan told you how she had to talk a client out of pulling his money after last year's party?"

He swallowed and nodded.

"I'm going to save you, but I need to go now." I handed him back his wallet and hurried toward the door. "I have salads in the refrigerator. I'll put everything out when I get back." I raced out and down to my car.

Thank God the Wegmans on Carlisle Pike was only ten minutes away. I parked in the lot and ran full tilt across the parking area and into the store. I barely slowed down until I reached the meat counter. "I need two dozen of those New York strips right there, and two dozen chicken thighs." With the hot dogs and hamburgers, that should be enough food. "I'll be back in five minutes to get them."

3

The butcher-counter man seemed as dazed as I felt. I hurried to the deli and got veggie and fruit trays, a shrimp tray, some coleslaw, potato salad, and pasta salad. Wishing I'd remembered a cart, I looked around in vain until one of the store associates took pity on me and brought one over. I thanked him and put everything into it, hurried back to the meat counter, where the butcher handed me the meat, and then raced through the checkout and out to the car. When I got back to Ronnie's, I had twenty minutes until the party started.

Ronnie stood outside the front door talking with two of the guys from the gym.

"Jerry, Bobby, give me a hand," I called and popped the trunk.

"What's all this?" Jerry asked. His eyes widened when he saw the food. "Thank God," he whispered. "No repeat of last year, I take it."

"Put the meat in the refrigerator and then find a couple of bowls. We can put the salads in them. Then get spoons—the serving spoons if you can find them."

"You got it," Jerry said. He hefted the packages as though they were weights. Jerry was maybe five foot six but built like a mini Hercules. He carried in what he could, and I got the rest.

"Is there change?" Ronnie asked, and I handed him three ones and some coins. His eyes bugged for a brief second, and then his expression returned to normal. "Thanks." Ronnie was like that.

"No problem," I told him and hurried inside. The guys were doing as I asked and had started setting out the food I'd purchased on the table, along with what I'd brought. I made sure the meat was in the refrigerator. I found the hot dogs and hamburgers in the freezer, so I transferred them to the counter to thaw for a while, wishing like hell I'd looked more thoroughly earlier. But they would be fine by the time cooking started in a few hours.

"Damn," Ronnie called.

I followed the sound of his voice outside. "What?"

"This is awesome, Clay," Ronnie said, looking over his table. "I should hire you to handle all my parties." I rolled my eyes and swallowed the quip that threatened as he threw an arm around my shoulder and yanked me into a hug. "I mean it. You really did save my ass."

I closed my eyes and did everything I could not to think about his ass, or how his arm felt against mine, or about the fact that he smelled like mild cologne, maybe some soap, definitely a touch of sweat, and that deep, low, earthy, spicy musk that I knew was all him. I moved away because the last thing I wanted was for Ronnie to realize that I was on the verge of full-on excitement just from the hug. He was only being friendly and appreciative, and I did not need him to freak out as guests began to arrive. "I'm glad to help."

"Ron-nie," a tall, young blonde said in a singsong way as she came outside. Her navy skirt, what there was of it, barely covered the subject from any angle, and her considerable assets were on full display in a white top with obviously no bra underneath. *Just Ronnie's type.* "Are you coming inside?"

"In a minute, Cherie," Ronnie told her. He released me, stepping back. She picked her way over in high-rise heels and wrapped an arm around Ronnie's waist, whispering in his ear. Ronnie made brief introductions, and I shook her limp-fish hand.

I shifted away from them. The perfume she'd bathed in had me on the verge of sneezing myself to death. Jerry and Bobby moved to either side of me. I glanced at them, stifling a smile. "Put your eyes and tongues back in your head."

Jerry nudged my shoulder. "That's easy for you to say."

I nudged him back. "Go open the garage and get the grill out and set up." I turned to Bobby. "You're the grill master. I'm going to go in and prep the meat before everyone gets here." The two of them hurried off, and I went inside, getting to work. I found spices and seasonings in the cupboard. Thank goodness one of Ronnie's exes had liked to cook.

"You know this is a party," Ronnie's mother, Dolores, said about ten minutes later as she came up behind me.

I turned, holding my hands away, but still got a kiss on each cheek. "And you know if I didn't help, everyone would go hungry or lapse into a sugar coma."

"Tell me about it. I nearly didn't come, because last year I almost starved to death." Her eyes blazed for a second. "I see Ronnie learned his lesson this year."

I stared at her for three seconds, tilting my head.

"You did it?" she asked.

"Yeah, I made him pay."

Dolores patted my arm. "You're a great friend. Ronnie is brilliant, but he has the common sense of a beetle, and let's face it, he thinks with his dick more than his brain. The man can make money grow like weeds, God bless him, but the rest...." She shook her head slowly. "But he's a good son."

"Ronnie saved me," I whispered and glanced over my shoulder. Her attention was elsewhere, and I didn't repeat what I'd said. Ronnie was also a good friend. I said nothing more for the moment. Dolores seemed to want to talk, and I didn't want to derail her train of thought. I returned to work as she leaned against the counter.

"I met someone," she whispered. "He's lived near me for some time, and he's really nice." She was clearly very nervous, and now I understood why. "I'm scared to tell Ronnie."

"I can understand that. In the sauna at the gym the other day, he was still lamenting the loss of his dad." Gary had died nearly two years earlier of cancer—from diagnosis to death was just six weeks.

"It's the OCD."

"I know. What others would process, deal with, and get over, gets stuck for him. But that obsessive-compulsive thing he does makes him a great investment manager and serves him and all his clients well. In many ways, he's turned it to his advantage, but when it comes to losing his dad, he can't seem to get past it. He knows he needs to, but he just can't. Not yet." I closed the first Ziploc bag with the steaks and seasoning and put the whole thing back in the refrigerator to marinate for a while, then began making up the next one.

"The thing is, I want to tell him about Eric, but...."

I thought about what to advise her while I finished seasoning the beef and put it away. More people were arriving, and the house was beginning to get loud. "If you want my opinion—and mind you, that's all it is—I suggest you wait until you know it's serious and a relationship that will last." I peered around the corner. Ronnie stood with another gym friend, Mark, and his wife, a local doctor. I'd had dinner with them and Ronnie after the gym many times. Ronnie was occupied, so there was no chance of him overhearing. "You know he's going to flip, so make sure it's worth it." I grinned. "And be sure to let me know when you're going to do it, so I can watch."

She threw her head back and howled. "I knew I liked you for a reason." She leaned closer. "Do you think Ronnie's serious about this girl? Or is it just a physical thing?" I had to give her credit—she had no illusions about her son. She had once told me about having the cabin next to him on a cruise ship and needing earplugs… for one night. After that she apparently laid down the law. Dolores was quite a woman. She had to be, with Ronnie as her son. He had no shame at all. "What are you going to do with the chicken thighs?"

"Just a little seasoning," I said. I opened the cupboard again and got out what I needed. "And a dash of heat." I smiled, knowing Ronnie loved spicy food. I added a little more Tabasco and worked the meat around until it was all covered. Then I sealed the bag.

"Mom, you old whore," Ronnie said, striding into the room. "There are some people I'd like you to meet." She shook her head and looked about ready to smack him. Ronnie was all about effect, and Dolores had heard Ronnie's smack talk before.

"My son, the smart-mouthed hound dog." She grabbed his ear for a second before letting him lead her out of the room.

"Is there anything else to do?" Jerry asked as he muscled his way through the gathering throng of people.

"I hope he got ice," I said.

"Ronnie said it was in the freezer."

"Then chill the beer." I began piling bottles of beer in his arms, and his face split into a grin. Jerry was in his early twenties and loved his beer. "There's also soda."

"I did that already."

"Great." I breathed a sigh of relief. "It looks like things are good, and we should be all set until we're ready to grill. The meat is marinating." I checked the hamburgers and hot dogs, then put them in the refrigerator to finish thawing. They would be fine when they were needed. "Go ahead and have a good time. I appreciate the help."

"It's Ronnie who ought to be appreciating you," Jerry said as he took the beer outside.

"It's what friends are for," I said to no one and then wandered into the dining room. I knew a number of the people there. I'd met several of them at the gym and others through Ronnie, who seemed to know everyone.

"Sweetheart." Dolores latched on to my arm as I passed. "This is Ted," she said with a brilliant smile. "He's been one of Ronnie's clients for years." For about five seconds, poor Ted looked like a deer caught in headlights.

I shook his offered hand as Dolores moved away.

"Not subtle, is she?" Ted finally said.

"Never has been in all the time I've known her," I told him, and then we stared a little nervously at each other. Ted was about my age, attractive, with a touch of gray in his black hair. "What do you do?"

"I'm a lawyer," he said and rattled off the name of the firm. Apparently I didn't react the way he expected. "It's one of the biggest and most successful firms in the state. Out of law school, I wanted to start my own practice, but that was a recipe for disaster. However, I was lucky enough to get offered an internship with the firm, and they thought my work was up to their standards, so they took me on after school, and now I'm a partner."

"That's...." I paused, trying to think of the appropriate term. "Impressive."

8

"Isn't it, though?" he said, and I realized I was in desperate need of alcohol. "But that's not why I told you all that."

"Oh?"

"Ronnie said you might need an attorney to handle some issues with your ex-wife."

Now the reason for the conversation clicked. And here I'd foolishly thought I was being set up.

I chuckled. "Sorry. My ex is a husband, and thank God we never legally got married." What a mess that would have been. "We talked about it a few times, but then things didn't work out."

"My firm helped establish some of the precedent in the state regarding GLBT law."

Now that actually was impressive. "Luckily for me, the house I live in was mine. We lived in his place and leased out the house I owned. It took a few months, but when the lease was up, I moved back home." I smiled. "He, on the other hand, didn't fare as well. Over the years I'd made improvements to his house, so he put me on the deed."

Ted grinned. "So you owned half of his house?" That seemed to tickle him. "Sounds like you have things pretty well in hand."

"Yes, sir, and he had to refinance to pay me off. Not that it was all that smooth, and in case you're wondering, Brian more than deserved everything he got. But if I do need anything at all, I'll be sure to call." I wasn't sure what else to say, and I felt like a stupid fool for my initial thoughts. "You never know when you'll need a good lawyer."

A woman not much older than Cherie approached Ted, carefully placing her hand on his shoulder. She was statuesque, with a smile that would light any room.

"This is my wife, Brandy," Ted said with an almost schoolboy smile. I saw both happiness and near childlike joy in his eyes.

"It's very nice to meet you," Brandy said. She shook my hand with professional ease and turned back to Ted. "I need you to meet someone outside," Brandy told Ted gently. "Would you excuse us a minute?" she said to me, and I nodded, watching them walk away arm in arm. I followed them out into the warm summer afternoon, where most of the guys I knew from the gym were gathered near the iced tubs of beer.

"Where's Ronnie?" Phillip asked.

Damn, these kids kept getting younger and younger every year. Phillip seemed like he was just out of high school. It wasn't true, of course. He had his own business and was reasonably successful. I knew it was me getting older, the possible gay-relationship clock getting louder and louder in my ears. Soon the bell was going to ring, and that would be the end. I'd be too old to date or for anyone to ever look at me with heat and passion again. And adorable guys like Phillip with perfect smiles, eyes like warm chocolate—and, from what I'd seen in the gym, abs to grate cheese on and a butt perfect for grabbing on to—and... I blinked to clear those thoughts. Phillip was gay, but at forty I was way too old for him. Not that I was interested in him particularly, just the idea of having a guy like him just once again before I shuffled off this mortal coil.

Phillip smacked my shoulder, waking me out of my wanderings. "Did you hear me?" He laughed, and the guys joined in.

"Give the guy a break. We have food because of him," Jerry said as he passed Phillip another beer.

"I saw Brian the other day," Bobby said.

Jerry nudged him hard. "Smooth, asswipe," he scolded. "Can't you keep your mouth shut? Clay doesn't need to hear about the guy Brian is dating." Jerry groaned. "Sorry, man. I should have just beaten the crap out of him."

"It's fine," I said. "We're not together anymore, and Brian can do what he likes."

"But, Clay...," Bobby began, and Jerry scowled him quiet.

"All right." I reached for a beer, popped it open, and drank the better part of the can. The guys watched me, wide-eyed. I rarely drank. "Tell me what's got you two so worked up."

"Well," Bobby said with puppylike enthusiasm, "I was downtown at one of the clubs. Not your kind of club... one with boobs and stuff." I rolled my eyes and kept quiet as Bobby got more and more uncomfortable. "Anyway, Brian came out of the steakhouse with this guy. We—Jerry, Ronnie, and I—said hello."

"Yeah. So he's dating," I said softly. "That's good."

"He was someone Jerry went to high school with." Bobby swigged his beer. "Hell, the guy was beautiful. I bet if I closed my eyes I could do him… as long as I could pretend he was a girl."

"I understood what you meant, and no one is going to impugn your straighthood." The air rushed out of my lungs. I got it. Brian was dating a much younger, better-looking guy than me. It hurt.

"The thing is, the guy leaned against Brian, grinning, and said that Brian had just proposed to him and that they were getting married," Bobby continued, and I damn near lost it. Yes, it had been a good thing we never married, but we'd talked about it, and Brian had always been the one who wanted to put it off. Now I understood he'd been keeping his options open, and at a fucking party the light came on. All the guys stared at me while I gasped for air. All the things I thought I'd known had been a lie.

"We know you thought you and Brian were going to be together forever. Man, you were like the perfect couple. At least most of us thought so."

"Who was the perfect couple?" Cherie asked, picking her way over in her heels. Jerry and Bobby both preened, and I was grateful their attention was elsewhere, so I could school my expression and get myself under control. It was hard. But I managed to do it, barely.

"We're talking about Clay and Brian. They broke up a while ago," Phillip explained to her.

She grew quiet and paled slightly. "How can you believe they were the perfect couple?"

Jerry and Bobby looked at each other and shrugged. "Clay's just one of the guys. So's Phillip. Just because they like dick doesn't mean they're any different from the rest of us." Jerry closed his arms over his sizable chest.

"It's not natural," she said and turned, hair bouncing as she hurried inside.

"What's not natural are her boobs," Phillip quipped, and the guys all broke into peals of laughter. "I was afraid her chest was going to explode, and we'd all drown in a sea of silicone."

Apparently Cherie's feelings weren't shared by many, including Ronnie, because she stomped out of the house a few minutes later, phone to her ear. "Yeah, Gus, I need a ride," she demanded.

Ronnie came out and joined the group.

"What's up with her?" I asked.

He shook his head. "You all having a good time?"

"Of course." To a man they lifted the glasses they were holding.

"We'll get the grill fired up soon," I told him, and Ronnie grinned. "The guys were just telling me about Brian."

"Shit, don't think about that cocksucker. No offense," he added hastily. "He's not worth it."

"I can't believe you didn't tell me he was getting married."

Ronnie put an arm around my shoulders. "Wouldn't have done anything but make you miserable. So forget it. The guy he was with was as plastic-looking as—"

"Cherie," I piped in, and Ronnie looked over at his one-time date. "Where did you meet her?"

"Internet," Ronnie answered without looking away, but I doubted he was actually seeing her. "A few weeks ago. I told her I was having a party, and she said she wanted to come." Ronnie pulled out his phone and began fishing through the pictures. "She's hot, right?"

"She sent you naked pictures? And you thought this would be a great person to meet because...?"

"She's young and hot," Ronnie answered as though that explained everything.

"Yeah, but is that what you really want?" I tilted my head to where Cherie stomped on the grass, heels digging into the turf. The thing was, she couldn't seem to figure out that the only way she was going to stop sinking in was to step off it. She looked like she was doing some crazy stomping dance. "The girl can't even figure out how to get off the grass."

Ronnie turned to me and opened his mouth but then closed it again. I knew a retort was seconds away, but he simply turned and stared at her.

"Besides," I said much more softly, "I heard you, remember? Was she just quiet or a dead fish? There's something to be said for someone who knows what they want and is willing to go for it with you, instead of lying there to let you do all the work while she stares out into space."

Ronnie's eyes darkened, and I realized I'd hit a nerve. Ronnie was always going for these young girls, but in the end they were only interested in what he could do for them. He came to that conclusion quick enough most of the time.

I figured it best to change the subject. "Guys, let's get ready to cook."

Jerry lit the huge, gleaming stainless-steel grill and closed the lid.

"I throw a great party," Ronnie said.

I cocked my hips slightly. "Please. *I* throw a great party. You have fantastic taste in friends. Everything you need to grill is in the refrigerator, and we should have food ready at about six." I turned to Ronnie, who nodded his agreement.

Jerry and Phillip headed over to the beer, because grilling was apparently thirsty work, and then got to it. I followed Ronnie inside and got pulled into a number of polite party conversations.

"The food is really good," a guest said a little later as he filled his plate.

"Clay took care of that for me," Ronnie said. Once their plates were full, Ronnie and the guest walked toward the back of the house. I had been to enough of these parties to know this was a chance for Ronnie to do some face-to-face business. The worst part for me was that I could always tell where Ronnie was. His laugh would drift over the conversation, or he'd sing obscene lyrics to a popular song, and of course his limericks were legendary. Not that I hadn't heard them all before, but he drew my attention, and I needed to get the hell over it.

13

I turned away from where Ronnie had gone and joined the group, got something to eat, and sat next to Dolores.

"This was wonderful, thank you for doing this for him," she said.

"Ronnie didn't put this together?" asked a man I didn't know.

I chuckled along with Dolores. "He got everything that could put you in a sugar coma. The rest I threw together." Thank God I was used to fixing problems at the last minute.

"He's a good friend," Dolores said as she patted my hand.

Dolores and I sat quietly while I ate, chatting a little and watching people as they came and went. Ronnie, of course, was in his element, and I sat back and watched a master.

After a few hours, people began to leave. Dolores said good-bye, and the diehards settled in. The guys from the gym stood outside talking and drinking. Others were sprinkled in the various rooms inside, also talking and laughing. I figured I would go as well.

I gathered up what little remained of the food. Most dishes were empty, so that was pretty easy. I left the rest out and went in search of Ronnie. I found him outside the garage showing his cars to a guest.

"I'm going to go," I told him and received a warm hug. I found myself closing my eyes and taking a short flight of fantasy before returning to reality. Ronnie was my friend, and that was all he was ever going to be. I wished I knew where this fascination had sprung from so I could cut it out and be done with it.

"I'll call you tomorrow and we can meet at the gym," Ronnie told me.

"Breakfast before?"

"Of course. I'll text you."

I hugged him again and then stepped back and walked to my car. I put the cooler back, which now just held my dishes.

In the car, I started the engine and sucked in air. It seemed to me I'd been holding my breath for hours, since the guys told me about Brian. For the millionth time, I wondered what I'd done wrong. We'd been happy, or so I thought, and affectionate. It wasn't like we'd been cold to each other. But apparently his feelings had an on/off switch, and I'd found out just how quickly they could change. I thought I'd been through all the stages of grieving—hurt, anger, hissy fit, revenge—and finally I could begin to move on. I guess I was wrong, because the hurt had stabbed me once again.

A rap on my window made me jump, and I nearly hit my head on the roof. After I caught my breath, I slid the window down.

"What's wrong with you?" Ronnie asked, sticking his head through the window.

"Nothing you need to worry about," I said softly. "You have guests to see to, and the fact that I can't seem to get over my asshole—"

Ronnie squeezed my face between his hands. "I'll tell you what you always tell me: 'Let it go.'"

I nodded, his hands smooshing my lips a little. "I'm trying. I thought I had." The words were garbled, and I closed my eyes, trying not to enjoy the way his surprisingly soft hands felt on my cheeks. It had been too damn long since I'd been touched in any way other than the socially acceptable handshake or guy hug. "What I can't understand is why you didn't tell me about him." I swallowed. "I trust you." I still did, because I knew he hadn't kept the information from me out of malice.

"Because I care," he answered. "And you didn't need to know what he's doing because it doesn't matter. His life isn't yours now." His brown eyes held gentleness. I didn't see that often in Ronnie. He was usually outgoing, loud, foulmouthed, and busy being the center of attention. "He's a fuckbag."

Now that was the Ronnie I knew. I nodded.

He pulled his hands away. "Go on, bro, get some sleep and try to forget about him."

"Who?" I said, my mind slipping off its normal track.

Ronnie grinned. For a second his milk-chocolate eyes captured my attention. "See? I'm helping already."

"Exactly." I figured I may as well play along. It would make him happy and cover up my momentary loss of attention. "How much longer do you think things will last?" I turned to where people were still talking in the light that spilled from the garage.

"Not much longer. I already told the guys I was going to work their asses like dogs in the morning at the gym, and that they were going to need their rest. The others will leave pretty quickly once they go."

I nodded. "I'm sorry about Cherie."

Ronnie shrugged and stepped back. "There was nothing there."

"Not since Maggie," I supplied. They had been together for two years, and the relationship had exploded six months after his father passed away.

He shrugged again. "I'm starting to think I don't know shit about women… or what the hell I want. Ever since my dad died, my life doesn't feel the same, and I don't know what's real. I thought Maggie was my rock, but she's gone too."

Ronnie's issues weren't solvable or even discussable in anything less than hours. Once he got hold of something, he didn't let it go. Many times I had wished there was some magic phrase or action that could snap him out of whatever he was obsessing about. For nearly two years, it had been the loss of his father. Everything in Ronnie's recent life related back to that one event. Long after everyone else would have moved on, he still held on as tightly as he could to that pain. Maybe that was one of the things we had in common: he with his father, and me with Brian.

"I promise I'll do my best to let go of Brian if you do the same with your dad and Maggie." I smiled.

"Deal," he said softly, vulnerability flowing off him. "See you tomorrow." He stepped away from the car, and I pulled out of my parking space, turning the car toward home while Ronnie stood in place, looking lost, until he faded in the darkness behind me.

CHAPTER 2

MY PHONE vibrated the following morning as I drove as fast as I dared toward the Panera near the gym.

Captain Cock, where are you?

Of course I couldn't answer him because I was driving, but Ronnie was most definitely back to normal. I arrived and found a parking space, walked inside, and found Ronnie, Bobby, and Jerry at a table.

"I got your usual for you," Jerry said. Damn, I hadn't realized I was so predictable. I sat down, and Jerry slid a bagel on a plate and an empty cup over to me. I went to fill up the cup with soda, then returned to my seat.

"Did you get everything cleaned up from the party?" I asked before taking a bite of bagel.

"The service is at the house now taking care of all that," Ronnie said as he pulled out his phone and passed it to Bobby. "That's the baseball card I'm interested in." He went into an explanation of card grading and rarity. When the phone got to me, I glanced at the photograph and tried like hell to keep from gasping.

"It's a bargain," Ronnie said. "Babe Ruth is always a good bet."

Only Ronnie would use the word bargain in reference to something priced at $32,000.

"Ronnie," I said softly and handed the phone back. He did this whenever he was disappointed about something. Extreme retail therapy was a normal behavioral pattern. When Maggie left, it was a Hublot watch, then a few weeks later a Lamborghini. Now it was baseball cards. "Just think about it, okay?" I kept my tone gentle. I knew this was just part of his OCD rearing its head once again.

17

"I think it's cool," Jerry said, adding his two cents. Bobby thankfully kept quiet. I ate my bagel in silence and let the conversation swirl around us as I worried about Ronnie. I liked to say that he was like the brother I'd always wished I had, but at some point, when I wasn't paying attention, he had become more than that to me.

"I think you should sleep on it, at least," I said with a smile.

"My dad and I used to collect baseball cards together," Ronnie said, as if that explained everything.

Jerry, Bobby, and I looked at each other.

"Your father is gone and has been for two years," I said. "People move on from loss and live their lives." I set down the bagel and glared at Ronnie. "I know what he meant to you, but you can't continue to fall back to this obsession with his loss."

"He was my father," Ronnie said firmly.

"Bobby, I know it was just you and your mother," I prompted.

"Yeah. Dad died when I was sixteen."

"You grieved and then moved on, right?"

Bobby nodded. "My mom was hit pretty hard, but we both grieved his loss, and after a couple years she started dating and then remarried. You've all met my stepfather. He's really cool, and while I still miss my dad, I love the guy, and he's good to my mom." Bobby smiled, and I thanked God he got what I was getting at.

"Bobby was a teenager when he lost his father, and he managed to get on with his life. You're almost forty years old and can't get on with yours."

"Fuck you," Ronnie swore quietly, but the fight I expected wasn't really in him.

"You're one of the best friends I've ever had." I ignored the other guys and locked my gaze onto Ronnie's, feeling a jolt of energy that I knew I shouldn't. "I don't want you to hurt any longer. Your father would hate it, and you know it. Gary was an amazing man who grabbed life by the balls and never let go. He was always there with a ready smile and a zinger to make everyone laugh. You know that." Gary had cracked jokes even the last time I'd visited him in the hospital, bald from chemotherapy, drawn, weak, and gasping for air. He'd used some of his last breaths to tell me a story about this farmer, his gay son, and a goat. I'll never forget the punchline: "Son, no matter what, remember, the goat... is female... so she's mine."

"Yeah, he was." Ronnie snatched up his iced tea and downed the last of it, then shoved his phone back in his pocket. After blank looks for a few seconds, he seemed to make a decision. "Are you ready to get beefcaked?"

I smiled and finished eating as Ronnie told us all what he was going to be doing at the gym today. By the time I was done, they had all come to an agreement about how ridiculous they were going to get in their workouts. I got up to fill my gym water container with ice, and then we all went to our cars and drove to the gym in the back of the shopping center.

I changed in the locker room while Ronnie talked to everyone. His big personality was back, and it was good to see. After filling my water bottle, I went up to the mezzanine to the treadmills. I got on one, dropped my phone into one of the cup holders, then started the machine and began my workout. I had a good view of the workout floor, so I watched as the others went through their routines, talking constantly as they did. A few times I saw Ronnie glance up, making the occasional rude gesture and then grinning like a naughty child. I was about to give him one back when my phone rang. I picked it up and answered it.

"Is this Clayton Potter?" I heard a strange voice ask.

"Yes, it is," I answered, figuring this was some sort of telemarketing call. I made a mental note to check the do-not-call lists.

"I'm Dr. Greenway down at Johns Hopkins in Baltimore. Your father listed you as next of kin. He was brought in earlier today. I'm afraid he's had as many as three strokes in the past few hours."

Hearing the word stroke, I forgot what I was doing or where I was. The machine kept working even as I stopped, and it pushed me off the back. I stumbled and managed to keep from crashing to the floor but ended up in a heap nonetheless as my legs gave out.

"Mr. Potter, are you all right?"

"I don't know" was the only answer I could form. My head buzzed and my ears rang, hands and legs tingling. "How is he now?"

"Howard is stable at the moment, but he's slipped into a coma. Part of it is the body's way of protecting itself. We need to run some more tests to determine the cause of the strokes, and then we may need to perform surgery to try to correct the blockage in his neck. Is it possible for you to get here? We will need permission to perform the surgery. I can do emergency surgery without it, but I would prefer we time this as best we can."

"Yes. I'll see about leaving as soon as I can." I stared at the phone, sitting on the floor while other people began gathering around me. I scanned the faces, people I didn't know all asking questions that didn't seem to register. Then Ronnie pushed his way in, and I took a deep breath as the fog over my mind lifted somewhat.

"What happened?"

"It's my dad," I told him. Those words galvanized Ronnie into action. He helped me to my feet and grabbed my things from the machine before turning it off.

"What happened to him?" Ronnie asked.

"Stroke," I answered. "Got to get to Johns Hopkins."

Ronnie stared into my eyes. "You can't drive. Not like this." Even as he said the words, he was already leading me down the steps and toward the locker room. "Change your clothes." He left me in front of my locker, and I stared at it, forcing my hands to work. I pulled off my gym clothes and got back into the regular ones. By the time I was done, Ronnie was dressed.

"Where are you going?" I asked.

"My dad was at Hopkins," Ronnie told me, and then he snatched up my bag and took me by the arm. My head was clearing, and the feeling was returning in my arms and legs, but I still felt shaky on my feet. He half propelled me toward the door, stopped at the desk briefly, and then we continued outside.

"My car is over there," I said, but Ronnie guided me to his and somehow managed to get both gym bags in the tiny trunk of the Lamborghini.

"I'm taking you down." He unlocked the car and lifted the door upward. It felt like I was still almost on the ground once I got in. Ronnie pushed the door down to close it and came around to the driver's side. As soon as he got in, he started the engine, which roared to life, and within minutes we were out of the lot and entering the freeway.

"You don't have to do this," I said, a little belatedly, though I was pleased he thought enough of me to take this much care. Ronnie and I were friends, but he was a very busy man whose time was extremely valuable.

"Of course I do." Ronnie reached over and patted my leg a few times, then returned his hand to the wheel. "When my dad was in the hospital, you came in all the time, talked to him and Mom." Ronnie's voice faltered for a few seconds. "She told me how you used to sit with her and just listen while she spouted all kinds of crap. Her words. She said she needed someone to talk with, and you were there." Ronnie continued driving as I stared out the window. I'd made the drive from Harrisburg to Baltimore more times than I could count. It had been just my dad and me for a long time.

"You know I used to have a younger sister," I said, letting my thoughts run wild. "She died when she was twelve. My mom died a year later. They said it was heart failure, and I know that was true. Losing Jeanine broke my mother's heart. Since then, it was just my dad and me."

Ronnie kept his eyes on the road and his foot on the gas pedal. "Remember I'm an only child too. Mom couldn't have any more after me. My dad and I were always so close. He was like my best friend."

"My dad is my dad," I told him. "He loves me, but he never understood me once I came out to him." I turned back to watching the scenery zoom by as Ronnie drove like a bat out of hell. I sure as shit hoped there weren't any cops around. "He didn't disown me or yell at me, but he could never understand that I would fall in love with men." I shrugged. "We still did things together, and he liked Brian. But even after all the years we were together, he still referred to Brian as my friend."

"Maybe that was how he could deal with it. My dad and I were close, really close, but there were things we didn't talk about. He hated Anne." I knew Anne was Ronnie's ex-wife, though I'd never met her. "He thought I was crazy for marrying her, and it turned out he was right. She insisted we wait to have sex, and then after we were married, she never wanted it. We slept in the same bed for years and nothing ever happened."

"Is that why you divorced?"

Ronnie pressed the brake as traffic nearly came to a stop once we got into Maryland. "Yes... well, no. We weren't compatible, and I asked her if it would be okay, since she didn't seem to want sex, if I could get it someplace else. That was a weird conversation and the point when we both realized it was over." He and Anne had separated a decade earlier, before I'd met him. "It was still the shits going through the divorce. We just wanted different things. My business was here, and she wanted to move back to New Jersey to be near her family. I decided then that I'd never remarry. I can't go through that again. Not with anyone."

It felt surprisingly good to talk about something other than my dad for a few minutes. It took my mind off him. But once Ronnie paused, the ache and worry fell back on me full force. I began chewing on one of my fingernails, nervously biting it as we got closer to the city.

"Stop," Ronnie told me. "Your dad is going to be okay. They can do wonders, and if something had happened, they would have called you."

I picked up the phone to check if I had missed a call. I hadn't. "I know, but...." I knew Ronnie understood, in his weird, obsessed way, more than anyone else I knew. Ronnie had only met my dad once, at a party I had a few years ago. They had talked, but they hadn't hit it off the way I thought they might. Both of them had drifted into conversation with others, and I hadn't understood why. Both my dad and Ronnie could tell a good story and loved to hear them. I had suspected they'd regale each other with their off-color jokes for hours. But the opposite had been the reality.

"Just keep thinking good thoughts."

I rolled my eyes as he threw my own words back at me. "Fuck you."

"See? Didn't help me then, and it doesn't help now. So I say that saying needs to be buried in the shitpile." He grinned. "Oh, and how about afterward, when people tell you he's in a better place?" Ronnie gripped the wheel. "I wanted to wring their necks."

That sent a chill up my spine, and I forced my mind not to go there. Dad was going to be okay. He was only in his late sixties—he'd retired just a few years earlier after working hard as hell all his life in the parts departments of car dealerships. He certainly deserved more of a retirement than a few years before it was all taken away from him. "I don't want to lose him. He's all the family I have."

Ronnie sped up, and we took the exit downtown. He knew exactly where he was going, and more than a few people gaped as we passed, going down the pockmarked streets in a car that cost more than many of them would make in a decade. He pulled into the hospital parking lot and found a spot. Then we got out, and Ronnie led me inside to a desk.

"Howard Potter," I told her. She clicked at her computer, then gave us each a colored wristband and told us he was in the ICU.

"I know right where it is," Ronnie said, and he guided me over to an elevator. "Are you going to be able to handle this?"

I nodded. "Sorry I freaked out earlier."

"You think I wasn't worse when they told me about my dad?" Ronnie asked. "If you remember, I drank half a bottle of whiskey and spent the entire night completely drunk and then puked all over the place."

"I do. Maggie called mad as hell and worried out of her mind. I told her to put you in bed with a bucket next to it and go sleep in the guest room." I pushed the call button for the elevator. "Only time I've ever seen you drunk like that."

"I don't drink," Ronnie said. "It interferes with the other medication. But that night…."

"I know." Hell, I did now more than I ever thought I would—the need to numb myself for what I was about to see. Some liquid courage to dull the worry would've been fucking helpful.

The doors opened and we got inside. Ronnie pressed the button for the floor, and we rode up and followed the directions to the appropriate section.

All the air around me seemed to have been sucked away as I stepped into the room where my father was. He lay still on the bed, breathing but not doing anything else, no other movement, eyes closed, machines hooked up all over. I was afraid to touch him in case I disturbed something. I stood at the side of the bed, staring down at him, silently willing him to wake up.

"I told the doctor that you're here," a nurse said as he came in. He was slight and kind of cute. I wanted to smack my face for having that thought while I was standing next to my dad, who was in a coma. "He's been resting peacefully since they brought him in."

I nodded. There was nothing he could tell me, though I had a million questions about my father.

"The doctor will be in soon to talk to you," he said as he moved through the room, taking readings and checking connections. I got the feeling he was keeping himself busy for some reason.

Ronnie moved into the room and came around me, sitting on the banquette in the corner. I paid him little attention, watching my father, wishing he'd open his eyes so I could look into them one more time. I needed to see my dad proud of me—the way he'd been when he was determined to teach me to ride a bike, told me how to do it, and I got right on and took off…. I reached for his hand and held it. These hands had built Pinewood Derby cars and showed me how to change my oil. These hands had made countless meals after Mom died, and these hands had hugged me and held me after Mom died. And the first time I got my heart broken, he'd thought it was over a girl, and I didn't tell him any different.

I closed my eyes and willed him to open his, sending all the energy I could out into the universe, hoping like hell it would come back to him. Things don't work like that, but I didn't care. It was worth a try. Eventually I ran out of things to say and think, so I walked around the bed and sat next to Ronnie, staring through the room and out into the hall but not really seeing anything.

"I can't believe you did this," I whispered.

"What, came with you?" Ronnie asked.

I nodded. "You wouldn't go with Maggie when she was running in that marathon in Miami, but you drove me all the way here. Because I needed you."

"She always needed me to go everywhere she was running and didn't understand that all I did was see the start and then go back to the hotel and wait for her to finish. It wasn't anything we did together. I was always proud of her and supported her ambitions, but I couldn't just sit around waiting all the time. That was what she needed: someone who would show her he loved her by being willing to wait. Instead, I showed her how I cared by including her in my life." He'd never talked about this. "I'm a selfish bastard about some things, mainly time. I never have enough, and that was all she wanted… and she wanted it all the time."

"Anyone you're with deserves your time and attention, no matter how busy you are," I told him, just above a whisper.

"Yes. But she didn't want to do anything without me and then got angry when I couldn't do all the things she wanted. Money I have in spades, and I spent plenty on her, but all she wanted was time." Ronnie turned and stared out the window. "The thing is, what first attracted me to her was the fact that she didn't want my money. Then I tried to buy her affections with it." He turned back to me, and I followed his attention to my dad lying in the bed. "He's going to be okay."

"How do you know?" I asked.

25

"Because I don't want you to go through what I did," Ronnie answered. I nodded slowly as a chill went through me. Ronnie must have felt it too because he hugged me to him, and I went with him, soaking in the comfort like a dry sponge drinks in the first drops of water.

The doctor walked into the room, and I had to give Ronnie credit. He continued holding me regardless of what the other man might have thought. I slowly got to my feet and approached while Ronnie stood behind me. It really felt as though he had my back.

"Are you Clayton?"

"Clay," I told him. The nickname had followed me from childhood, and I had decided years earlier that I was going to own it rather than try to change it.

"Joseph Greenway." We shook hands. "Your father's strokes were brought on by blockages in the arteries in his neck. I'd like to schedule surgery for tomorrow to try to remove them. Without the surgery he'll most likely have another stroke and die because of a lack of blood flow. However, it's also possible he won't survive the surgery."

"So it's damned if we do and damned if we don't," I said.

"If we can clear the artery and restore blood flow, then the strokes should stop, and he'll have a chance to recover."

"All right." It didn't sound as though I had much choice—either a slim chance or no chance. "When will you do it?"

"I'll get him on the schedule for first thing in the morning."

I took my dad's hand. "Okay. Have them bring in whatever consent forms they need signed, and I'll take care of it." I'd do whatever I had to for him, but the doctor certainly hadn't given me much hope.

"I'm sorry I don't have better news for you."

"I appreciate your honesty." What else was I supposed to say? I had wanted a completely different message, but I wasn't going to get it.

"We'll prepare him first thing, and there's no need for you to be here all night. He isn't going to wake up, and we'll keep him as comfortable as possible."

I nodded blankly. "Thank you." We shook hands again, and he left the room. I stood near the bed, still holding Dad's hand, not knowing what I was going to do if he didn't make it.

"It'll be okay, Clay," Ronnie said from behind me.

I wanted to yell at him for the platitude, but what was the point? "I'm sorry to take you away from everything."

"Don't worry. Just spend time with your dad. I'm going to see if I can find us both some coffee and something to eat."

Ronnie left the room, and I moved closer to my dad. I sat quietly for a while before I figured I might as well tell him what I wanted to say. There was a good chance he wouldn't survive the surgery, and I'd heard that sometimes people could hear things in a coma, so I thought, *What the hell?*

"Dad, it's been just you and me for a long time now. I know that after Mom died, you always did your best, but it was hard for you too. You'd lost a daughter and then a year later your wife. I always wondered why you never dated again, and I think I may have the answer now. Just like I didn't want another mother, you didn't want another wife because Mom was the best. She took care of all of us, and I...." I wiped my eyes. "Losing Jeanine broke Mom's heart, but I wish you and I had been enough for her. We deserved to be." It was an old hurt but one that felt good to voice after all these years.

"But you were always there, coaching Little League, which I sucked at. Boy Scouts—at least you and I had fun doing *that* together. You even took me camping and fishing. We didn't have a lot of money, but you made up for that with attention and time. You always had that for me, and somehow—I have no idea how you managed it—you sent me to college. You said you'd swing whatever it cost. For all I know, you mortgaged the house to pay for it." I inhaled deeply. "The thing is, we never talked—not about what was really important. You used to tell me stories, and that was how I got to know you, but they were stories you made up for fun, not the ones I really wanted to know. Like, I wanted to know if you felt as lost as I did sometimes. Now I think you did, and that's why you didn't talk about it. You didn't want to unload on me."

I sighed. "Dad, I want you to get better even for a few days, so we can talk to one another the way we should have. I want a second chance... for both of us." I squeezed his fingers slightly, then placed his hand under the covers and sat back down.

Ronnie came back in the room and handed me a cup of coffee and a bag. "Here, I brought you this. There wasn't a lot that wasn't fried or dripping in fat. It's a bagel dog."

"What did you get for yourself?"

He shook his head. "I'm fine for now. I had a protein drink down there, and that will tide me over. I also got a hotel in town, so you can stay close." He glared at me. "I know what you're thinking, and stop it. I'll be with you tonight, and tomorrow we'll see what happens." He squeezed my arm, and I lifted my head, saying a small prayer of thanks for the best friend possible.

I hadn't realized how hungry I was until the food hit my stomach. I finished the bagel dog, wrapped the trash, and tossed it away. "I don't know what to do now," I said softly, standing once again beside my dad's bed. There were people I needed to call. I pulled out my phone, though for some stupid reason I couldn't get a signal unless I was near the window. I pressed my dad's sister's number. "Aunt Dorothy, it's Clay."

"I can tell something's wrong," she said right away.

"Dad had a stroke, and right now he's in a coma." I went on to explain what the doctor had said.

"Do you want us to come?" she asked.

"You can if you want, but the surgery is first thing tomorrow morning, and you're a day's drive away." I didn't think it was practical. "The best thing you could do is call the rest of the family for me, and I'll keep you informed about everything that happens." She lived in Michigan, and it was at least ten hours by car. I knew making flight arrangements on this short notice would cost more than she could afford on her fixed income.

"Are you sure?"

I swallowed and turned away from Dad, looking out the window. Even though it was unlikely he could hear me, what I was about to say seemed traitorous. "The doctors aren't giving me much hope. So all we can do is pray." Going into contingencies was more than I could bear, so I left the rest unsaid.

"All right. I'll make the calls to the family here." She paused, and I heard her sniffle quietly. "I hate that you're alone."

"I have a good friend who's sitting here with me. He'll be here through the surgery."

She cleared her throat, and tension filled the connection between us. I knew she wanted to ask exactly what kind of friend he was. She had never accepted that I was gay. The concept was outside of her ability to understand, I knew that. Dorothy was caring, and I loved her very much. After Mom died, she was the one I would go to when I had questions I wanted to ask a woman. But once I came out, it was like there was a corral around certain parts of my life that she simply couldn't deal with.

"Ronnie is a good friend. I think you met him and his ex-girlfriend the last time you came to visit." I figured even if she hadn't, the ex-girlfriend part was what she wanted to hear. There was no use fighting with her, so letting her off the hook was the easiest thing for all of us.

"That's good. I'm glad you aren't alone." She sniffled again. "Let me know right away if anything happens."

I promised I would, and we ended the call. As soon as I let the phone drop away, I blinked a few times to keep the tears at bay. All of this was so overwhelming. Dad should have so many good years left. "It's just too soon, Dad," I whispered.

I used my phone to look up the number for my dad's old employer and remembered one of his old coworkers, who by chance was still there. I told him what had happened, and he promised he'd let the men Dad had worked with know. After that I called some old family friends and then dropped the phone on the cushion. The walls were closing in, and I needed some fresh air. "I'm going out for a minute," I told Ronnie.

"Do you want me to come with you?"

"If you like." I figured roaming the halls would burn off some of the excess energy. Ronnie stood, and I walked to the door. He stayed behind for a few seconds, and I saw his lips moving silently. Then he looked up and joined me. "You okay?" I whispered.

"I think that's what I should be asking you."

I swallowed hard. "This hits close to home for both of us." Ronnie nodded. We silently left the room. I stopped at the nurse's desk, told them that I was going for a walk, and made sure they had my number. They assured me that he was stable for now and that they would call if anything changed.

Ronnie led the way to the elevators and then down to the main floor. The hospital was a maze of departments and halls that went on forever, intersecting with others that also seemed to go as far as the eye could see. We didn't talk, and as my nerves ramped up, I moved faster and faster. Ronnie kept up with me until sweat broke out on the back of my neck. Then I slowed and stopped, wondering where in the hell I was.

"Let's head back. We're on the other side of the hospital," Ronnie told me. He turned and led me back. "You know, whatever happens, it's going to be okay. I bellyache sometimes, and I miss my dad, but it will be okay." Ronnie stopped walking and turned to me. "After the funeral there were times when I wanted to die. I thought about taking my own life more than once." He blinked a few times, and I yanked him into a hug, cradling his head in my hands. I expected him to pull away, but he hugged me back. "It was the meds and the OCD going overboard. I know that now, but I felt like I couldn't go on."

"But you could. We were all there for you. I was there."

"You were, and I remember you coming over, watching television with me."

"You were in bed, and I...."

"You lay next to me for hours. We didn't talk, just watched television."

"As I remember, it was car racing or something." I released him and stepped back.

"I knew that day that you loved me," Ronnie said, and I stiffened. Had I been so transparent? "You're my good friend, and I love you for that. I found out who my true friends were after my dad died."

"I know." I'd seen him cut people out of his circle after that. They just seemed to disappear.

Ronnie began walking again. He didn't talk, and for that I was grateful. Some time alone with my thoughts was appreciated, but too much would drive me out of my mind. We reached the elevator and took it back up to the ICU floor.

Dad was the same, lying still. The machines beeped and made lines on the screens, displaying various numbers that I didn't take the time to understand. I visited with Dad, talking to him about nothing important. I figured we might as well catch up, so I told him what I'd done since the last time we talked on the phone. When I ran out of things to say, I sat down on the banquette and stared at the wall. Fatigue caught up with me, and I leaned over, resting my head on the top of the cushion.

The room was too warm, and I knew if I could get a little cooler, I'd fall asleep. The beeps at some point turned rhythmic and eventually melodic and lulled me just a little deeper. Eventually my mind let go, and I dozed off. I woke a little later to find Ronnie cradling my shoulders, his chest a pillow for my head. "Sorry."

Ronnie humphed and didn't make any effort to move. It felt good like this. He was warm and smelled muskily good. His strength was like an anchor that held me in place. I closed my eyes again and didn't move, pretending to be asleep once again, just so I could be close to him.

The nurse coming in the room roused me and I sat up, yawning and forcing my weary brain to something that resembled coherence. He went about his work, taking readings and staring at one of the monitors. Then he turned and strode away. A few minutes later the doctor came in, and the two of them had a soft conversation.

"Is something wrong?" I asked.

"No. Just the opposite. We're seeing more activity. I want to get him down to surgery just as soon as I can." The energy in the doctor's voice gave me hope. "Let's not wait." He left the room, and it became a hive of activity as they got Dad ready and then wheeled him out.

"You can wait here or in the surgical waiting room," the nurse said. "Just let us know where you'll be."

"I will," I said. I turned to Ronnie.

"There are probably chairs and sofas in the surgical waiting room. They're definitely more comfortable than this," he said. I followed his advice, and we shifted to the waiting room.

I SPENT hours getting intimately acquainted with the surgical computer printout. I knew my dad's room and the progress of the surgery by watching the timeline fill in. I got no word from anyone, but I took that as good news. I fidgeted to the point that Ronnie wanted to smack me repeatedly. I could see it in his eyes. But then I wanted to smack him sometimes too, so I figured we were even.

"How much longer do you think it will be?" I asked, not expecting an answer.

"Hopefully soon," he told me.

After staring willfully at the monitor for ten minutes, the line for my dad's procedure went green, meaning it was done. My heart caught in my throat, and when the doctor came out, I held my breath and Ronnie's hand.

"He came through as well as I could have hoped. The blood flow is really good now. He's in Recovery, and we'll keep him sedated for the rest of today and tonight in order to allow initial healing to progress as far as it can. Then in the morning we'll pull back on the medication and see if he responds." He looked as weary as I felt. "I suggest you go on home and try to get some rest. Come back first thing in the morning." He smiled and turned away.

"I guess we better go," I said to Ronnie.

"No problem. I'll take you to the hotel, and then we can eat."

Dad was alive and the surgery had gone well. Now it was out of our hands, and all I could do was pray.

RONNIE TOOK me to dinner, then disappeared to the hotel gym. I settled on one of the beds, watching television and sinking into my own thoughts. I hadn't even realized how much time had passed until Ronnie returned. He went right into the bathroom, and I heard the shower run.

The water shut off and then the bathroom door opened. Ronnie strode out with a towel wrapped around his narrow waist. I had seen Ronnie naked many times because he was shameless as hell, and that shone through tonight, because he pulled the towel away, tossed it into the bathroom, and slid into the other bed. I honestly tried not to look, but I watched each and every movement.

I slid off the bed and took my turn in the shower, trying not to think of Ronnie naked just outside the bathroom door. It was impossible. I wished I'd brought clean clothes in with me, but I ended up leaving wrapped in a towel. Thankfully the room was dark, so I dropped the towel next to my bed and climbed in. I tried going to sleep, but I knew Ronnie was in the next bed, naked, and my mind began conjuring up scenarios that I shouldn't have been thinking.

"Clay," Ronnie said from the other bed.

"Yeah," I said warily.

"You know…," he started suggestively, and I had a very strong suspicion where this was going.

"Ronnie, you and Cherie were going at it yesterday. Remember?" The man was a horndog of the highest degree.

"Yeah, but the bird is awake and raring to go."

"Ronnie, you're straight," I told him, even as my heart rate sped up slightly.

"Yeah, but you could come over here and suck me off. It's dark, and I'm sure you know what you're doing." Ronnie's voice was low, and it didn't take much of my imaginative energy to realize what Ronnie was doing in the other bed.

I rolled onto my side, barely able to see Ronnie's outline in the other bed. "Jesus," I groaned under my breath. I could easily jump into his bed and get right down to it, blow Ronnie's mind, and then go back to bed. But I valued myself more than that, and I knew if I started, I wouldn't be able to finish with that. It was best if I just rolled over and pretended I hadn't heard anything.

"You've seen what I have, and I know you like it."

That was about as unsexy a thought as I could possibly imagine. "You sound like really bad porn, you know that?" I forced a laugh to try to diffuse the energy that crackled in the room.

"Isn't that what you guys like?" he wisecracked.

"No. Actually it isn't. I'm not into anything bad." I sat up. My eyes had adjusted enough that I could see his hand slowly sliding up and down. Holy fuck! It had been way too long since I'd had sex, and dammit all to hell, I couldn't look away. I dramatically threw back the covers and sat on the edge of my bed before shifting over to Ronnie's. "You know," I whispered, leaning close enough that I was sure he could hear me, "over the years you've told me a lot of things I doubt you intended to."

"Oh yeah?"

"Uh-huh. I remember what you said Maggie used to do so you could come."

"The medication I take interferes with—"

"Maybe," I said as I leaned closer. "Maybe it was just what you liked. Maybe it wasn't a finger you were wishing was deep inside you, touching that spot." I watched as Ronnie stopped the slow stroking. "Maybe what you wanted was the real thing. Because you don't know much about me when it comes to what I like in the bedroom."

"I assume you like to get fucked."

I reached across and slid my hand over Ronnie's chest, slowly plucking a nipple. I heard his breath hitch and then a moan built in his throat. "I don't, Ronnie. Not particularly. What I like is to be the one doing the fucking." God. I clamped my eyes closed. I couldn't believe

I was saying all this right now. This entire situation was fucked up beyond belief. "Is that what you want?"

"Ummm...."

"That's what I'm offering. I'll take you to the moon and back." I slid my hand down his belly and then along his hip. Ronnie quivered under my touch. Damn, it was so hot, and I prayed he didn't ask me to stop. "Your head will spin, and your eyes will roll to the back of your head."

"Fucking hell," Ronnie breathed, and I slowly climbed onto the bed, sliding my hands gently up Ronnie's ankles and calves.

"Is that what you want?"

"I...." Indecision was clear in his voice.

"You have to say it. If you want me to drive you to the top of Everest and then higher yet, make you wish your head would explode, then you have to say it." His legs shook under my hands, and as I slid them up his legs to his inner thigh, the muscles shook as though he'd just had the workout of his life. Then I stopped, my hands midway above his knee, not moving at all as I waited for his answer. My heart raced faster than I could ever remember. This was the chance I had wanted for so long. It was dark and this would probably be a one-time thing. Ronnie could easily change his mind in the cold light of day, but now, in the dark, with just the two of us, if he wanted me, I'd give him the best of what I had.

"God, I...."

I slid my hands back down his legs. "If you want me to go back to my bed, just say so."

Part of Ronnie was indecisive, but a part of him jumped against his belly, stretching a good way toward his belly button.

"No," he gasped. "I want...."

"You have to say all of it. You have to say you want me to fuck you," I breathed, saying the words I knew could very well make him pull back and tell me to stop.

"Yes, do it," he said.

I knelt between his legs and slowly bent over him. "This isn't something you need to endure or grit your teeth over." I placed both hands on his chest. "And if it's that little voice in your head that you're warring with, just turn it off. As long as we both feel good, that's what counts. Not what anyone else will think."

"Okay," he breathed.

"Good. Now take a deep breath and then slowly let it out." As he did, I made little circles on his chest and then down to his belly, then along his sides.

"Aren't you just going to fuck me?" Ronnie asked.

"My God. Are you like this with women? Always itching to get to the end? Just relax and I'll take you to a place you'll wish you could never leave." I leaned forward, feeling where Ronnie's cock stretched long and thick. Whatever battle was going on in his head, his dick certainly knew where it stood. I inhaled deeply, his scent driving me forward.

I licked up his length, teased the base of the head, and then backed away.

"God," Ronnie breathed, his belly rising and falling.

I sucked the head between my lips, and he thrust his hips forward. I pushed them back, holding him still.

"I'm in charge for now." I took him deeper, and Ronnie whimpered softly, his cock throbbing between my lips. It didn't take long for me to realize just how Ronnie liked it: hard and fast. So I was deliberate and slow, keeping him on the edge. I knew exactly how he felt by the way he breathed and the soft flow of expletives that rolled off his tongue.

"That's damn good," Ronnie said as I took him deep and held him there, my nose pressed to his manscaped skin.

"I know," I told him when I needed to take a breath. "You already told me."

"When? How?"

"By the way you breathe and that small moan that you try to stifle but can't. Just let go and stop worrying." I sucked him deep once again and used my knees to lift and part his legs. Once Ronnie was gasping and begging, approaching the edge, I pulled back and slipped off the bed.

"What the hell?"

"Just breathe and close your eyes. I need to get some things. I'll be right back." I hurried to the bathroom and grabbed what I needed from my kit, then returned and got back on the bed, slapping Ronnie's hand away from his cock. "None of that. Not tonight. I'll make you come so hard you'll swear you died and went to heaven, but we do this my way."

I dropped the condom and lube on the bed and got back into position. Then I leaned over him, my lips inches from his. Without asking or thinking, I crashed my mouth onto his, taking possession before he could stop me. It took two seconds before he returned the kiss, which surprised the hell out of me. Ronnie wasn't a good kisser; he was a hot as hell, curl your toes kisser and gave as good as he got.

I pulled back, gasping for air, then sucked down his neck and to a nipple, teasing the hardening bud with my lips and then scraping lightly with my teeth. He shook under me, pressing his chest forward in an unmistakable signal. I searched the bedding for the lube and found it as I bit lightly.

He wrapped his arms around my head, pressing me closer to his chest. "Fuck, yeah."

I opened the lube and stilled my lips, lessening the sensation. I had him riding a roller coaster, and as soon as we reached a dip in the track, I opened the bottle and slicked my fingers. I moved to the other nipple, scraping, licking, and sucking on it, and as he cried out, I slipped a finger inside him.

Ronnie stiffened until I found the spot I was looking for. He growled and nearly came off the bed. I smiled at him and stilled my finger, sucking him at the same time. I knew what Ronnie liked—what most guys liked. When I stilled again, I turned on one of the bedside lights to the lowest setting.

"What's that for?" Ronnie asked.

"No matter what, you are going to know who you're with. No pretending." I added a second finger, prepping him for what was to come later.

"I wasn't," Ronnie told me. "I know who I'm with."

"Good." I scissored my fingers, twisting, and watched as he dropped his head back on the pillow, mouth hanging open. Damn, he was such a hedonist, getting lost in the sensation. By the time I pulled my fingers away and rolled on the condom, he was breathing hard again, his eyes wide. He said nothing, but I felt him retreating. With the condom in place, I wrapped my fingers tightly around his cock and slowly stroked along his thick, silky length, my grip firm and sure. When the glassiness of pleasure returned to Ronnie's eyes, I got into position and slowly pressed into him.

He gasped as the head of my cock breached him. I gripped his cock harder, stroking faster, pressing a little deeper. I knew that within seconds the pain would morph to pleasure, and I counted to five and then slid deeper.

"Fucking hell!"

"I know, and you haven't felt anything yet." I pressed deeper, working his cock firmly. When he tried to bat my hand away, I gripped him tighter. "I know you know yourself best," I told Ronnie, "but I want you to lie back and know that I'm going to bring you off." I stilled and felt his body grip around me hard. "Damn, you're tight."

"You think I do this all the time?" Ronnie countered. He reached for the bedside light, switching it off. I thought about telling him to leave it on, but I let him have it his way.

"No. But you feel amazing." I wrapped my arms around his neck, pulling him up into a deep kiss. "You're an amazing man, and you have no idea how fucking hot you look right now." I snapped my hips and kissed him, angling my cock to scrape along that spot inside him. He gasped and cried out, biting my lips slightly. I kissed him hard, thrusting deeply as Ronnie began to unravel beneath me.

He wrapped his arms around my back, grabbing at me as I thrust harder and faster. I backed away and stroked firmly. Ronnie writhed under me. I knew I was close as tingles and warmth began at the base of my spine, spreading through the rest of me. Within seconds I was holding back my own release, determined beyond measure that Ronnie tumble first.

He whimpered, and I twisted my hand as I slid it along his shaft faster. I thrust harder, slipping into the zone where my mind began to fly.

"Holy fuck," Ronnie growled between his teeth, hissing and moaning constantly just before he tumbled over the edge, coming all over his belly and my hand, heat searing my skin wherever his release touched me. I followed right behind him, shaking along with my release as tiny lights flashed in the darkness.

I stilled, afraid to move as long as the light haze of afterglow lingered around me. I couldn't believe what had just happened. I blinked in the darkness, checking that I hadn't been dreaming. Ronnie breathed deeply below me, sweat acting as a slick glue wherever we touched. This was surreal. I'd dreamed of being with Ronnie for quite a while, and now that it had happened, I nearly shook with fear. I gently pulled out of him and slowly climbed off the bed. I went into the bathroom, took care of the condom, and used the dim nightlight to stare at myself in the mirror, wondering what in the hell I'd just done. Wanting something and then getting it felt amazing, but I couldn't help wondering what the cost would be, and if in the end I would get my heart broken and lose my best friend all at the same time.

How long I stood in front of that damned mirror I didn't know. Once the near panic passed and my breathing slowed from a pant to something approaching normal, I turned on the water and grabbed a cloth and a towel. I wiped my hands and did a quick cleanup before opening the bathroom door to face the music.

The room was silent, only Ronnie's soft breathing letting me know he was even there. I walked to his bed, and he started when I used the warm cloth to clean him up. He said nothing, but I could feel him staring at me in the darkness. I didn't want to look at him for fear I'd see the rejection—or worse, hatred—in his eyes for what we'd done.

I dried him off and put the cloth and towel back in the bathroom. When I returned, I stood between the two beds, wondering what in the hell I should do. I wanted to get back in bed with Ronnie. His comfort would have meant so much, but dammit, I didn't know what he wanted.

"Are you just going to stand there like a moron?" Ronnie asked sleepily.

"No. But…." I shifted my weight back and forth nervously and took a step toward my bed.

Ronnie lifted the sheets and moved over on the mattress. I took that as a signal and got into the bed. Ronnie pulled up the covers, then lay still. "Fuck it all to hell," he groaned, rolling over. "Don't analyze this, because I don't know what to think right now." He tugged me to him and his warmth spread through me. "Just go to sleep and hopefully all this shit will make sense later."

"Okay, if that's what you want." What the hell else was I going to say?

"Go to sleep, Clay," Ronnie told me.

I wanted to, but I stayed up most of the night while Ronnie slept, alternating between concern that I'd just lost my best friend, fear of losing my father, and hope that maybe, just maybe, I hadn't actually lost either of them.

CHAPTER 3

I SLEPT very little, but I must have eventually dozed off. When I blinked myself awake the next morning, I was alone in the bed and heard water running in the bathroom. I rolled over and smelled Ronnie on the sheets next to me. The scent of the gods. Worry slammed into me a few seconds later, and I got out of the bed and hunted down my gym bag. At least I had clean underwear. I had started pulling them on when the bathroom door opened.

Ronnie stepped into the room completely dressed. He stared at me hard, and I turned away, unable to deal with the recrimination and hatred I was sure I was going to see.

"It's your turn in the bathroom. We need to be dressed and ready to go soon."

"Okay."

"I called down to the desk and asked them to send up razors and toothbrushes. I left yours in the bathroom." Ronnie busied himself packing his things, and I grabbed my pants, shirt, and gym bag and retreated to the bathroom, closing the door.

I couldn't breathe at all. Leaning with my hands on the counter, I gasped for air, trying to deal with what I knew had just happened. "I have to think of my dad first," I whispered as I pushed all the other stuff from my mind. That was what was important right now, not how stupid I'd been last night. I wondered if I could somehow pass the whole thing off as grief, pain, and worry, tell Ronnie I was sorry and that it shouldn't have happened. But, Jesus, even in my head that sounded lame on top of lame, and Ronnie didn't deserve a bunch of platitudes to try to explain my complete stupidity. I busied myself getting cleaned up and dressed. I hated putting on my dirty pants. There was a clean T-shirt in my bag, which helped me feel less grungy. Once ready, I held my breath and left the bathroom.

Ronnie was packed and ready, sitting on the edge of the bed. I pulled on socks and tied my shoes, trying not to look at him, but of course I failed and saw him looking back at me a few times.

"Are you ready?" Ronnie asked, and I stood, grabbing my things. We left the room, heading to the elevators.

During the ride down, I wasn't sure where the hell to look. The walls threatened to close in, and then, to my relief, the elevator doors finally slid open. Ronnie went to the desk, handing in the room keys. When I pulled out my wallet, he threw me a look so cold it stopped my arm still. Well, at least I had my answer about how he was going to react. I needed to get used to the fact that things between Ronnie and me were never going to be the same.

I stepped back and waited until Ronnie was finished, then followed him out to the car. The sun was just lightening the sky as we drove the largely quiet city streets to the hospital. He pulled into the main drive and in front of the doors instead of going to the lot. "I'll be up in a little while," Ronnie told me, and I unlatched the door, letting it rise upward before getting out of the car.

"Okay," I said, and then I closed the door. Ronnie sped away, and I watched the car turn onto the street before I headed inside. I had to keep my thoughts where they belonged, with my dad. I inhaled the crisp summer morning air before I pushed through the doors. I checked that my father was in the same room, then did my best to remember the route we'd taken.

I managed to find the room just fine. A nurse stood beside his bed, adjusting one of the monitors. Dad looked exactly the same, though maybe he had more color. It was hard to tell, but any sign of hope was welcome at this point.

"You need to put on a gown and gloves to help prevent infection after surgery," the nurse said. I set down my bag and did as she instructed. I left my bag out in the hall next to the cart because of the dirty clothes and such, and entered Dad's room.

I leaned over the bed and carefully took his hand. "How are you today, Dad?" I whispered. "They said they were going to reduce the medication, and I hope to God you wake up." It felt good to talk to him, whether he could hear me or not. "I stayed in town. My friend Ronnie was here yesterday. He got us a hotel room, and it was super fancy. Ronnie never does anything halfway."

"Talking is good," the nurse said as she came in. "I'm Cindy, and your dad and I will be together for the day." She chuckled and wrote her name on the whiteboard near the sink. "The last sedative was administered a few hours ago, so it should be working its way out of his system."

"That's good," I said, still holding his hand.

"It is. But if he wakes up, it isn't going to be one of those dramatic moments like in the movies where he'll open his eyes and five minutes later everything is hunky-dory."

"I know. Because of the stroke, he could have brain damage or…." My imagination started to run away with me, and I closed my eyes to stay under control.

"We don't know anything right now. So don't get yourself worked up. We learn here to take things one step at a time." She patted my shoulder and then went back to her work. "Praying sometimes works too."

I chuckled. God and I hadn't been close in quite a long time. My aunt and all her preaching and using the Bible as a weapon for anything she didn't agree with or understand had left me with a fairly cold feeling about religion in general, but I said a short prayer regardless and then sent my aunt a text message to let her know that Dad had come through surgery all right and that he was still unconscious. I also asked her to call me. She was an early riser most of the time, but it was too early to call nonetheless.

I sat on the sofa, settling in to wait, and ended up staring at the wall. My mind played an energetic game of tennis, bouncing back and forth between worry about Dad and recriminations about what had happened with Ronnie. I heard Ronnie outside the room, talking and joking with one of the nurses, and then he strode in with some coffee and a small bag of what smelled like donuts.

"I wasn't sure what you wanted." He handed me the container and lifted out his own cup of coffee before sitting down next to me. "Anything so far?"

I shook my head. "The sedatives were stopped a few hours ago, so all I can do is wait and hope." I sipped from the cup and pulled out one of the donuts, then bit off a piece. It tasted like sawdust in my mouth. I was sure there was nothing wrong with it, but nothing, including the coffee, tasted right.

"I know all about that," Ronnie whispered. He sipped his own coffee. He sat next to me, but he felt a million miles away. I sat back and closed my eyes, wondering what in the hell I should do.

"I'm sorry," I finally whispered, not knowing what to do to bridge the Grand Canyon on the cushion between us. Maybe it couldn't be saved, and I'd screwed things up between us forever.

I felt Ronnie lean closer. "If that apology was for what happened last night, so help me I'll punch you so hard they'll need another bed next to your dad's."

"Huh?" I asked softly. "I thought…."

"You know I can obsess over shit better than anyone—it's one of my gifts." He smiled and then glanced down at his lap. "That's another of my gifts, if you know what I mean."

I smiled and wanted to smack him at the same time. "Sometimes you're an ass," I whispered.

"And sometimes you assume you know exactly what everyone else wants."

"So you're okay with… what happened last night?" I raised my eyebrows questioningly.

Ronnie shifted his gaze toward the bed. "We'll talk about it later, once I've had a chance to think."

"More like obsess over it," I countered.

"If I had to guess, I'd say that you're the one who's obsessing over last night, and I'm telling you that there are more important things right now. We'll talk later. I just need a chance to think about what happened, and you need to spend all your energy and attention on your dad."

He was right, of course, and I held my head in confusion. I'd gotten carried away last night, taking solace in Ronnie's arms and using him to try to forget about my dad. At least that's what I tried telling myself, but the words rang hollow in my head. "You don't hate me?"

"No. I don't hate you." Ronnie tilted his head toward the bed, and I went to my dad, taking his hand once again and pushing the other distractions away. It was Dad who was really important now, not me and what I'd done to complicate my life. That would all still be there once....

"I don't know what to do," I said softly.

"You were always an active child," my dad whispered, the words slurred. At first I wasn't sure I'd heard what I had. Dad's eyes were still closed, and I'd barely seen his lips move. Other than the few words, there was no other sign he was awake.

"Dad, was that you?" I asked, but I got no other sign and no answer. "Did you hear him?" I asked Ronnie, who shrugged and shook his head. "He said something."

Ronnie came over and stood next to me. Dad didn't look any different, and there was no other response. I left the room and found Cindy, then led her back to the room. "He said something to me a few minutes ago."

"Mr. Potter, can you hear me?" Cindy asked. There was no response or movement. She tried again and then looked at the monitors. "I can get the doctor, but I don't see anything different. Sometimes we want to hear or see something so badly that we think we do."

"I didn't imagine it," I told both of them.

"Okay," Ronnie said. "Then what did you do?"

"I whispered 'I don't know what to do.'" I watched, but Dad didn't respond this time. "Before, he said 'You were always an active child.'"

"All right. Keep trying, and if anything else happens, let us know." I think she wanted to believe me but was torn, and I had to admit that I wasn't sure I'd heard what I thought I did.

But Ronnie clapped me on the back and grinned. "I believe you. I heard once that Mel Blanc, the guy who did Bugs Bunny, was in the hospital in a coma, and they'd all given up. Someone said 'Hey, Bugs' or something like that to him, and he answered in Bugs's voice. That part of his brain was active while the rest wasn't. From there he began to come out of the coma. So if you triggered something in him, try again. Ask him questions," Ronnie suggested.

"Dad, can you hear me?" I asked, lightly squeezing his hand. "That's me holding your hand. Clay. If you hear me, squeeze, just a little." I waited but didn't get so much as a finger movement. "Do you remember when you used to take me camping? We used to go to that lake up in the mountains. The water always felt so good in the summer heat." Dad didn't respond. But I continued. "I used to go down to the lake—"

"You spent all day in the water," Dad rasped softly, and I turned to Ronnie, who nodded. It hadn't been just me who heard it that time.

"Yeah. I stayed in the water all day, and when it rained we used to stay in the tent—"

"We played games for hours."

"Go get the nurse," I told Ronnie, and he hurried out of the room. "Yeah. I used to beat you at Monopoly and Yahtzee all the time. But now I think you used to let me win."

"I never did," Dad said as the nurse came in.

She stopped dead and grinned. "I'll call the doctor."

"You're talking to me, Dad. The real me. This isn't a dream or some delusion from the medication. It's me, and you need to open your eyes and look at me." I motioned to Ronnie, and he turned off the lights and then went over to the window and pulled down the curtains. "It's nice and dark in here, Dad. Nothing is going to hurt your eyes." I leaned over the bed, still holding his hand and lightly stroking his cheek. "Come back to me, Dad. I need you as much as I ever did."

"No, you don't," Dad whispered.

Mom always said that there was no mistaking whose son I was: all she ever had to do was look into my eyes. She said I had Dad's blue eyes, and I never believed her until I saw my father's eyelids lift and I was looking into them. Yeah, they were the same ones I saw every morning in the mirror, and when I looked into them I didn't know whether to break down in tears or smile. I settled on a grin. "Welcome back, Dad," I said softly.

"It is you," he whispered, and I swallowed hard, reaching back. I found Ronnie's hand and squeezed it. He would later tell me that I nearly broke it I grabbed him so hard, but he never said a word at the time.

"Mr. Potter, it's good to have you with us again," the doctor said from the other side of the bed. "You gave us all quite a scare. I'd like to check your eyes and look you over for a few minutes, and then we'll let you talk to your son." He looked to me. "Don't worry if he falls asleep."

I nodded automatically and turned back to Dad, who lay still, looking back at me and blinking.

"How long have I been here?" he asked. He was still slurring his words, but he sounded a little stronger.

"A couple of days," I answered. "You had surgery on your neck, and they got the blood flowing again, so you need to rest and let that heal, but you're going to be all right now." Dad was awake and talking. The worst was over. It had to be. I stepped back and let the doctor check what he needed to. I sat down next to Ronnie on the sofa, leg bouncing with excitement. "It's going to be okay," I whispered.

"He's going to be fine," Ronnie reassured me, and I could feel Ronnie's loss ring jealously in the words. I knew Ronnie didn't mean me or Dad any harm; it was just that he wished more than anything that he'd gotten a second chance with his dad.

"Thanks to you," I told him.

"What did I do?" Ronnie asked.

I gaped at him. "You were here. You brought me down when I couldn't have made it on my own. You stayed with me." I hugged Ronnie. "You're a good friend, and I know how valuable that is." The thought that I could have messed all that up last night was more than I could even think of. I needed Ronnie as a friend almost as much as I needed air. Yes, I'd wanted more—and I still did—but putting the dear friendship that I desperately needed at risk....

"So are you," Ronnie told me, and I breathed with relief. He and I could go back to where we'd been. We could leave what had happened last night alone, incorporate it into our friendship without letting it ruin everything. I got what was left of my coffee. It was pretty much cold, but I didn't care. I was suddenly both hungry and thirsty. I finished off the donuts and the rest of the coffee, then threw the packages away.

The doctor left, and the nurse was about to when I stood and saw my dad lying still once again. "Don't worry, he's sleeping now," the nurse said. "He'll do that on and off, but it's just healthy sleep, and he's going to need a lot of it."

"Okay." I wondered what I should do now. I turned to Ronnie. "Maybe if you take me to Dad's, I can get his car and you can go home. I know you don't want to sit around here and wait for me."

"I can do that if you like," Ronnie agreed. It would also give me a chance to get some things that Dad might need. "Why don't we wait until your dad wakes up so you can tell him where you're going? That way he doesn't wonder what happened to you." He settled back and got comfortable. "I'm not in a big hurry."

"Thank you." There was so much wrapped up in those few words. My throat tightened, and I found I wasn't able to say more, even if I had words to say it.

I sat back, alone with my thoughts, until I heard Dad softly ask for me. I spent a few minutes talking to him, answering his questions and putting chips of ice between his lips. I wondered if those first drops of water were painful, but after that it had to feel good.

"Ronnie is going to take me to get your car when you fall asleep, and then I'll come back. I'll stay at your place for a few days."

"What about work?" Dad asked.

I'd completely forgotten and ran through my projects in my mind. Things were under control, and the computer systems I was managing the installation of could continue without me for now. "I'll call in, and they'll understand. I have enough vacation and personal time that I don't have to worry. What really matters is that you're going to be okay." I lightly squeezed his hand. "So if you need to rest, just go to sleep, and I'll come back as soon as I can."

Dad waved his hand slightly. The nurse came in, and I explained where I was going. She brought him some juice and said that they were going to see if Dad wanted to eat anything in a little bit. I helped him drink some and then left the rest on the tray.

It was hard saying good-bye, but I did, and then I followed Ronnie out of the hospital and to the parking lot. "I can't tell you how much everything you've done means to me." I settled into the seat as Ronnie pulled out of his spot. People walking to their cars stopped to take a look at the exotic car.

When we turned out onto the road, I let my mind wander back to Dad. I hated being away from him. Then I turned and looked at Ronnie, wondering what he was thinking.

"All right, I think we need to talk," he said.

"About last night?"

"No, about frying fucking chicken," Ronnie snapped. "Of course last night. I mean you... we.... You know me, I'm not ever at a loss for words, but I don't fucking know what to say. We... well, you fucked me, and I liked it, so does that make me gay all of a sudden?"

"No. Some people might think so but no. You really like women, so you might be bisexual, but being gay or straight is about the person you fall in love with, not who you have sex with. The thing is, how do you feel about it?" God, I was scared shitless Ronnie was going to say he hated me for it. He was almost forty years old. To discover something like that about yourself would be shocking for most people, but to realize that at forty could be world-shattering.

"I don't know." Ronnie pulled to a stop. "I mean, I love a good blowjob and all that, but I damn near passed out when—" He began moving again and grew quiet for a moment, then said, "I can't believe I let you fuck my ass, and I can't believe how amazing that made me feel, but I don't think I'm gay. I like tits way too much."

"It doesn't really matter. You're just you."

"Well, shit, that's really helpful," Ronnie groused. "Leave it to you to come up with some touchy-feely crap when all I want is an answer."

I shrugged. "I can't give you one. I know what last night means to me, but I can't know what it means to you or what you want to do about it. We could simply forget it ever happened, and you could go on with your life the way it was before. This doesn't have to be some huge deal. So we had sex. It's not like I'm going to tell everyone about it."

"You're not? I thought…."

I growled. "Quit stereotyping."

"Fine," Ronnie huffed. "I'm trying to figure all this out, and you're not helping."

"There's nothing to figure out if you don't want there to be." I turned to look out the window. "Okay, I'll try to be less… like you." I had to grin at that.

"Smartass."

"Okay. Let me ask you, what do you want to happen?" I turned back to him as we got on the freeway. "Do you want a repeat of what we did last night?" I expected a vehement no and got silence. "Do you want to give up women and make a life with a man? Do you want to chalk last night up as an aberration because you were trying to comfort me because of the impending loss of my dad?" I sighed and waited for him to answer, but all I got was silence. "Like I said, last night doesn't need to mean anything." At least to him. I knew without a doubt that I would carry the memory of being with Ronnie for the rest of my life. If we were never together again or never spoke about it again, I'd still remember the way he quivered under me, the way his breath hitched, and the way those moans filled my ears and touched my heart. I should have thought about what I was doing more carefully. I knew that now. I had pressed Ronnie into doing more than he was ready for, and now I'd kicked off a crisis of identity that I hadn't been prepared to help him with.

"I don't know what I want," Ronnie said plaintively.

"You know that's okay too."

"How is that okay?"

"Ronnie, you just discovered a part of yourself that you didn't know about. You're forty years old, and you didn't know that you could be with a man and enjoy it. Most guys would never have had the guts to explore that part of themselves. I've always known you were a strong personality, but to know that under the bravado, vulgarity, and quick wit is someone with more courage than I've ever known makes me proud to be your friend." I closed my eyes and tried to stop the damn tears from welling. I shouldn't have been acting like that, and I chalked it up to everything that was happening with my dad. I turned to stare out the window once more.

"Okay, but what do I do now?" Ronnie asked.

"I don't know what to tell you. Go home and do what you normally do. Troll for chicks on the Internet if that's what you want. Pick up more girls like Cherie and bring them back to your place for a night of fun and let them think they're going to get something from you. I don't know. You could go out to the clubs and pick up all the guys you could want. They'd flock to you."

"They would?" Ronnie asked in that "little kid in a candy store" way he had sometimes, and I couldn't suppress a chuckle.

"Of course they would. You could also go home, watch television, or go to the gym and meet the guys the way you do every day. Then you could go to dinner, and tomorrow you get up and go to work, and when things get intense, have a stress-ball fight with John. Nothing needs to change that you don't want to change. This is your life, and you're the one in control of it."

Ronnie didn't respond. Other than me telling him where to turn, we remained silent, just the hum of the tires, engine, and road filling the car. By the time we reached my dad's condo, I was exhausted and strung tight with stress. I'd messed up bad. I should have stayed in my own bed and not done my thinking with my little head.

Ronnie pulled into a parking space, and I got out. "Do you need anything?" I asked.

"No," Ronnie said quietly, staring straight ahead.

Shit, I didn't know what to say. I wanted to make him feel better, but I didn't think that was possible at the moment. "Thanks for everything. Having you here with me…."

"Anytime. You know that," he said softly without turning his head. "I better head on home." Finally, he turned in my direction. "Be sure to call me later and let me know how your dad is doing."

I promised I would and stood back while Ronnie backed out of the spot and then pulled away, out of the condo complex. I watched as he left, then pulled out my keys and went inside. I knew my relationship with Ronnie would never be the same. That wasn't possible now. Sex changes things. But at the moment, I didn't know if things were going to be better between us or if I'd lost the best friend I'd ever had. The one friend I could ask about things like this was Phillip, but I wasn't going to say a word to him. If Ronnie wanted to forget about what had happened, I sure as hell wasn't going to tell any of the guys. They could be as gossipy as old biddies. No, I'd brought this on, so I had to pay the piper.

CHAPTER 4

I SPENT nearly a week with my dad, using vacation time, buying what I needed, and doing laundry a lot. Each day he got better and his strength built. Now that blood flow had been restored, he improved on a daily basis. He wanted to go home, but in the end, he left the hospital and went to a rehabilitation facility where they could help him work through some lingering weaknesses and speech issues. I visited him in the rehab center in the morning and said good-bye, telling him I'd be back down to see him as soon as I could. Then I told him I loved him, and he'd hugged me tight.

He'd called a number of friends already, and some had been in to see him, so I had little doubt that Dad would have plenty of visitors while he was in the facility. The hard part had been arranging a way to get back home, but I'd hit on a stroke of luck. Phillip said he was coming down to Baltimore to do some shopping, so he met me at my dad's and we rode back up to Harrisburg together.

"Is he going to be okay?" Phillip asked as we rode.

"Yes. It looks like this has been coming on for a while, but the surgery did him a lot of good. There's always the chance that the blockage could return, though." I hated that thought, but there was nothing I could do about it.

"They didn't say it would happen, did they?" Phillip asked. I shook my head. "Then don't worry about it." He smiled as we zoomed down the freeway.

"You drive faster than Ronnie," I commented as he passed another car.

"I know. My dad says I should have been a NASCAR driver. But I just hate the time in the car, especially when it's the same drive I make all the time to see the folks. If there's something new to see, that's okay, but this is always the same." He did slow down just in time to pass a police car waiting by the side of the highway.

I wanted to ask about Ronnie and find out how he was doing, but I was afraid to. He hadn't called or texted while I was gone, and that made me nervous. Ronnie usually texted me every day, even if it was just to confirm that I was going to the gym, but for the past week, there had been nothing at all.

"I understand," I said to Phillip, trying to remember what we'd been talking about.

"You okay?" Phillip asked.

"Sorry, just worrying about Dad," I lied. Well, fibbed a little. I had been worried about Dad, but not at that particular moment. "He's going to be fine, but I hate leaving him alone in that facility. I'd hoped we could bring him home before I had to leave."

"How long will he be there?"

"A couple of weeks. I'll have to come back down to help him move back home, but I think they'll be able to help him." Many times I had wished I lived closer to him. "It should be good, though. He's looking forward to getting home, but they'll take good care of him and make sure that when he goes home, he can take care of himself."

Phillip nodded. "Have you talked to Ronnie at all?"

"Not since he returned home. I suspect he's been busy." I tried to keep my voice normal, and I was glad he'd brought up the topic. "Is something wrong?" I cringed as soon as the question crossed my lips.

"I don't know. He's been subdued for the past week, like he was after his dad passed away."

"He was with me, and I know being around my dad affected him."

"It isn't that. He's seemed different somehow. Quieter. You know how he is in the sauna—loud, teasing everyone, and talking the entire time anyone is in there with him. Yesterday, he sat quietly, like he was thinking about something." Phillip shook his head. "You know how he shaves all the time because he can't stand the hair on his chest and back? Well, this really hairy guy came in, and he said nothing."

"Huh?" I asked. Ronnie was always telling the hairy guys they should shave. It was one of his favorite things.

"Yeah. I doubt he actually even saw the guy. I thought he might have been sick or something. You know he's a huge baby when he's sick." Phillip chuckled to himself, and I watched out the window. "It's funny how well we all know him."

"How can we not? He's just one of those personalities that gets in your face, and there's no duplicity in him. What you see is what you get."

"That's just it. There's something he's been chewing over, and he isn't talking about it. Jerry tried to talk to him about it, and Ronnie bit his head off." Phillip slowed down again, and I turned away, cringing to myself. I knew I was the source of Ronnie's short temper and introspection. Why couldn't I have simply stayed away from him? "It's like his OCD is on overdrive, and he can't control it. Though that usually results in him talking more."

"So you're really worried about him?"

"Sort of, yeah," Phillip said. "You can see for yourself tomorrow morning. He asked when you were coming back, and I told him I was going to give you a ride back today. That was yesterday, and after that he got quiet again. Bobby thinks he's off his medication, but Ronnie takes it religiously. We hoped you'd be able to talk to him and find out what's going on."

"Okay. I'll see what's going on." I'd call Dolores if I had to, but at this point, Ronnie needed time to think and figure things out. But I wasn't going to say anything about that to Phil.

"He talks to you about things a lot more than he does with the rest of us," he said. Phillip glanced over at me, and my mouth dropped open. "He does. Ronnie jokes and gets to be the center of attention with the rest of us, but he tells you things that he doesn't tell anyone else. You were the one who wasn't shocked when he and Maggie broke up."

"Yeah, but that didn't take him saying anything. They'd lost interest in each other, and regardless of how it came off, the breakup was inevitable. Ronnie just didn't want to see it, and Maggie had to be the one to leave, for both their sakes. They were on a track to make each other miserable, but Ronnie was never going to kick her out. He'd just complain about her to everyone who'd listen. If you listened to him, you'd think she went from being an angel to the devil incarnate, but that's just his OCD talking. He can't let go of anything, including her, even if it wasn't working."

"See, you know all that stuff," Phillip said.

"It's because I'm old and you're not." God, there were some days I felt ancient.

"Is that why Ronnie always tries to date girls who are way too young for him?"

I laughed. "No. Ronnie doesn't see himself as growing older. In his mind he's still in his twenties, so he wants to date girls in their twenties, but then they drive him crazy because they're immature. And the ones who will go out with him always want something, though he's too smart to be taken advantage of. If you want the truth, he isn't going to be happy until he finds someone his own age to care about."

"You think so?" Phillip slowed behind some trucks going uphill, and I bit my lip at the way he squirmed behind the wheel.

"Take it easy. Getting back five minutes earlier isn't worth an accident." I smiled, and Phillip eased off and sat back. "Yeah, I do think so, but he doesn't see himself with anyone his own age, so that isn't likely to happen soon."

"Unless he met someone attractive."

"No. It's going to take a very strong person to be able to cut through some of the Ronnie bullshit, and most people aren't willing to do that. Unless they want something."

"You mean like Miss Silicone 2015 from the party?"

I laughed. "God, I wish I'd thought of that. Yes, she probably wanted to be seen hanging on Ronnie's arm while he drove her around in the fancy cars, took her to all the best restaurants, and bought her jewelry. And for that she was willing to put out." I settled back in the seat. "I wish he'd realize what he needs and would allow himself to be happy. But the grass is always greener... or in his case the boobs are always bigger and the ass is always higher on the next girl to come along."

Phillip laughed. "You're hilarious."

"Thanks," I said. I noticed Phillip looking at me in a way he never had before. "What?"

He turned back to the road. "Nothing. I guess I never really noticed you... that way before. I mean, you're an attractive guy and all, but... I guess I never really looked at you as anything more than a friend."

"That's because it's what we are." Phillip was an adorably handsome kid with eyes that could light up any room and energy that would be mind-blowing in bed. He reminded me of the Energizer bunny, and while that might be fun to take for a spin, there was no way I could ever keep up with him. "You're an amazing guy, and when you meet the right one, it will be awesome." I was surprised he wasn't beating them off with a stick.

"So you aren't interested in me?" Phillip said.

I was floored by the turn this conversation had taken. "I'd be a fool not to be, but I'm way too old for you. Not just because I'm almost fifteen years older, but because you deserve someone who has that same drive and spark that you do, and someone who can keep up with you."

"I've been out with lots of guys, but nothing ever happens," Phillip said.

"When I was a kid there was a song—'Looking for Love in All the Wrong Places.' Is that what you've been doing?" Phillip didn't answer right away, but he didn't deny it either. "You aren't going to meet Mr. Right at a bar. Only Mr. Right Now goes there, and believe me, there are plenty of them. Let me impart some of my old-guy wisdom." Phillip smiled, and I continued, wondering if I should be hurt that he didn't say I wasn't old. "We all go through the looking-for-sex phase. First we come out; then we go out with everyone we can find. Eventually we realize we want more. So change the places you look. Join a club. There are plenty of guys at the gym. The thing is, go out with a guy, on a date, that doesn't end in sex."

"Like dinner and a movie?" he said with disbelief.

"Sure. Go on a date. Ask a guy out and have a good time. Take him to dinner, make him dinner, watch a movie, whatever. And at the end of the night, say good-bye, kiss him good night, and close the door. There's something to be said for doing things the old-fashioned way."

"Okay. And what if he thinks I'm nuts?" Phillip asked.

"Then he wasn't the right guy, and you'll find someone else. If you've been out with a lot of people, then you know there's always more fish in the sea. And sometimes those buggers stink to high heaven when you get them out of the water." I held my nose, and Phillip giggled. "So if the guy winds up stinking, throw him back."

"That's easy for you to say," Phillip countered.

"Why, because I'm older? That means the fish have had more of a chance to age and get even stinkier. Most of the good men are happily making families with men they've been with for years. And guys like me, who are between relationships because they got thrown back, are only in the sea for a very short time before they get caught by someone else. So all I can do is keep looking and hope I meet someone. The same as you. At least you've got all your hot cuteness going on to use as bait. My bait got bit a long time ago."

Phillip giggled once again. "Okay, you're funny."

"It's either laugh or cry, and I already did more than my share of crying. So I hope someone nice will come along." I'd been hoping that for a while.

"So why not see… you know, with me?" Phillip asked, and damn if I could give him an answer that made sense. Phillip was cute, and I wasn't exaggerating. He had classic good looks, and that smile…. If he worked as a miner, he wouldn't need a lamp. Everything was perfect about him—except that he was so young and had his entire life ahead of him.

"You need to build your life. Meet someone, fall in love, get your first place together, have the grand adventure and romance so that when the hard times strike, you have all that to fall back on. Think about it. When I walk into a room, does your heart stop and your mouth go dry? Do you wonder if I'm going to come over and talk to you? Do you hang on every stupid word simply because you want to be near me all the time?"

"No."

"Then that's why. You deserve to have that, and you shouldn't settle for anything less. Just go out and find him."

"Okay. But...."

"I'll also tell you to find some different friends. You hang around us all the time, but you aren't going to find anyone that way. Jerry and Bobby don't know anyone, and Ronnie will only scare potential gayboys away or ask to see their birds and they'll do it."

"Yeah, I know. I had a date last year, and we stopped by. Apparently Ronnie asked to see his bird, so he showed him. I hadn't even seen it yet, and he was waving it around for Ronnie."

"And...?"

Phillip giggled. "Ronnie did me a favor." He burst out laughing, and I hoped to hell he stayed in control of the car. "Apparently, the guy was—"

"I get it, and he was willing to show it to anybody and not particularly fussy. Yeah. You know I'm not saying to stop hanging out, but find some other people too. You have to have younger friends who are gay. Ask them to introduce you to people. They already know you, so you might get lucky."

"Is that how you met Brian?" Phillip asked.

"No. Well, kind of, I guess. We met in Provincetown. I was staying as a guest of a friend of Brian's. He'd rented a house for the week and we were sharing expenses. Turned out Brian and I ended up sharing more than either of us expected. He was from Kentucky, and I was from Baltimore, and we had this long-distance thing that went on for a while. Then I got my project management job in Camp Hill, and he got a job with the state as a historical preservation specialist, and we ended up here. He moved in, and everything was great for almost seven years." I didn't want to get maudlin, so I stopped there. "Sometimes things happen. I wasn't expecting to meet anyone and had gone to P-town because I had the vacation time and someone backed out of the house rental."

"Do you regret it?" Phillip slowed down as we approached the final turnoff at the end of the Harrisburg side of the freeway.

"Surprisingly not. If I had it to do over, I would. Brian was dynamic and so much fun, at least at the start. He had the same kind of energy you have, and it was attractive. In bed he was a live wire and just—" I stopped and let the memories wash over me. "Things changed over time. Our jobs demanded more, and we let them become what was important. But we were happy together, and things were good most of the time. Yeah, he turned out to be a shit in the end, but...." I shrugged and grew quiet. There wasn't anything else to say.

He drove me back to the gym to pick up my car.

"Thanks for everything." I leaned over and kissed him on the cheek. "You're a great person, and you'll find someone who makes you blissfully happy." I wished it could have been me in some ways. He was young, vibrant, and if I could keep up with him for a while, it would be an amazing ride. "I'll see you soon." I opened the door and got my bag from the backseat. It was stuffed full with the clothes I'd ended up buying for my stay.

"I'll see you tomorrow at the gym."

I nodded and waved as he pulled out of the parking lot. Then I drove home, walked up the flagstone walk to the front door, and let myself in the house.

Mail spilled out onto the floor from the slot. I set my bag down and gathered it all up, carrying the whole mess to the kitchen. I plopped everything down and got to work on the chores that had been neglected. Everything in the fridge was exactly as I'd left it, only a week older, so I threw away what had started to smell and got the trash outside to the can. Then I took care of anything else that needed immediate attention and called my boss at home to let her know I'd be back to work on Monday.

Once all the chores were done, which took a few hours, I was at loose ends. I could watch television, but I didn't want to. I thought about calling Ronnie to see what he was up to, but I was afraid. That was all I could say. I was too scared to hear what I was sure he was going to say. I ended up going outside and puttering in the yard for something to do. It was sunny and warm, and the fresh air helped clear the cobwebs and the smell of disinfectant and hospital from my system.

"Having fun?"

I looked up and saw my friends Greg and Barry out on one of their afternoon walks. They were also friends of Brian's, but during the split they'd decided they liked me more and made their affections known. I stood and took off my gloves, motioning toward the patio in the shade. They followed me, and I excused myself and went inside, then returned with a pitcher of ice water. "This is all I have in the house. I haven't even had a chance to make some tea yet."

"This is great," Barry said as he gently sat in one of the chairs. Greg took the one next to him and patted Barry's knee. "Just what I needed on a day like this."

I poured myself a glass and took the remaining chair. Barry and Greg had been together for decades and were both retired. Ronnie had managed their money for years, to their great benefit, apparently.

"How is your dad?" Greg asked.

"In a rehab facility. But it's a miracle—it looks like he's going to recover most of his functions. He'll probably always need a cane for balance, but he can talk pretty well, with less slurring every day. Ronnie took me down to the hospital, and he stayed with me through the worst of it."

Greg and Barry shared a meaningful look and then returned their attention to me. They both drank their water, with unreadable expressions of curiosity—at least that was the best way I could describe it.

"What's up, you two?" I asked.

"Well, we were wondering what Ronnie's deal was. We know he always has the Barbie dolls on his arm, but he never seems that interested in them. We went to lunch with him before his party. We were invited, but after last year we made sure we had plans." Greg rolled his eyes.

"I arranged for decent food this year," I told them, and Barry shook his head.

"Anyway," Greg interrupted with one of his wry grins. "When we went to dinner, he had this Cherie with him, but he pretty much ignored her, even when she practically shimmied her fake boobs in front of him. We've always thought he was...."

The temptation was so great to tell them what happened between Ronnie and me. Their advice would be helpful, I was sure of that. But there was no way I could do that to Ronnie. If he chose to ignore what happened between us, then I would respect his wishes. "I've only ever seen him with women, and you know Ronnie—he's always after the next pretty young thing. He's that way with cars, and women too, I guess. After the divorce, Maggie was the only one who could keep his attention for long."

"That may be true, but I think he goes through women because he's trying to find something he never will with them," Barry said. "He doesn't need what those women have to offer. He just thinks he does."

"What does he need, then?" I asked.

"He needs the strength of a man who knows what he wants." Barry drank his water and stared at me.

"He's straight," I said with as much vehemence as I could muster. "I don't think he can change his orientation any more than I can change mine."

Greg leaned forward. "I doubt sexuality is as black and white as we'd all like to think. Yes, there are guys like Barry, who are gay and being with a woman is impossible. Me, I'm closer to the middle. I'm gay, but I was with women and everything worked just fine. I know people who are truly bisexual and have had long-term relationships with both men and women. Dale is a friend, and he was with Peter for almost twenty years. After Peter died, he met a woman, and they seem happy." Greg shrugged. "Everyone is different, and I think Ronnie may be somewhere in the middle of the continuum."

I knew that was a definite. The question was, what side would Ronnie allow himself to come down on?

"Ronnie needs to figure out for himself what will make him happy." Lord knew I wished I could make him choose me, but in his business and world, it would be difficult for him to decide he wanted to be gay. He could lose clients—large clients. Yeah, most people wouldn't care, but if clients started deserting him, it could result in a snowball effect. I worried about him. In some ways Ronnie was strong and powerful, but in others he was fragile, and that vulnerability had been evident in the death of his father.

"So you agree with us?" Barry asked with delight.

"What does it matter? He's free to live his life the way he wants. How can we or anyone else say different? We've been fighting most of our adult lives for the rights we're due." Marriage equality had reached Pennsylvania the previous year, and Greg and Barry were some of the first to take advantage of it. They'd marched together in rallies for years fighting for gay rights.

"Of course it doesn't matter what we think," Greg said. "But it is fascinating. Ronnie struggles with a lot of things in his life. You know that probably more than anyone."

"Phillip said almost the same thing on the way home. But I don't think I understand him any better than anyone else does. He doesn't tell me much more than he does others." I tried to keep my expression neutral.

"But he does. And you watch him the way you watch everyone." Barry placed his glass on the table beside his chair. "It's what you do. At a party, you talk to people, but you watch everyone. You see how Ronnie reacts to people, and you know when he's interested and when he isn't."

That was true. I'd learned as a scrawny kid that threats could come from anywhere, so watching the people around me gave me an advantage. When someone was angry or drunk, I'd be gone so when they lost control, I wasn't in the line of fire.

"Has he ever said anything to you?" Barry asked.

I shook my head and tried to think of a way to change the subject. "Do the two of you have a trip planned soon?" They loved to travel.

"Thailand," Barry answered with a grin. "We're going to Bangkok and then out from there to see the temples. It should be amazing. Then we're traveling to Myanmar. We don't usually do tours and things, but we've always wanted to go there, and the country has opened up enough now that they are welcoming tourists. There are places few Westerners have ever seen, and we want to be among the first to see them." They were like excited children, so I sat back and let them tell me all about it.

"Then we're going to Vienna and Prague next spring," Gary said. They had obviously each picked a destination. Their interests were varied, and I was a little jealous to hear them talking about all the places they were going. I would have loved to have been able to travel like that.

"Ronnie wants me to go on a cruise with him this winter. He keeps trying to get a whole group of us together to go." Shit, I'd brought the conversation back to the topic I'd been trying to steer it away from. "I'd like to go. It would be nice to get away from the cold in January."

Barry finished my thought. "But it would be nicer if you had someone to go with."

"That and I'm worried about my dad. What if something happens while I'm away?"

"I know you're worried, but you can't stop living your life. I doubt your dad would be happy about that." Barry was right, of course. "Besides, you'll have a good time. Just talk to your friends and find one who'd like to go."

What I really wanted was someone to share the cruise with, not just a roommate. But that was unlikely to happen, and I needed to make alternate plans if I wanted to be able to spend some of January in the warmth and sun. "I will."

Barry and Greg stood. "We need to finish our walk, but we're putting together a dinner party for next month, and we'll contact you."

"That would be great," I told them, and we exchanged hugs. Then the two of them left the yard, and I picked up my gloves, bouncing them on my hand. The urge to garden had passed, and I ended up putting everything away before going inside.

I showered and lay down on the sofa to watch television and rest for a while. I was watching an antique-hunting show, just seconds from dozing off, when my phone buzzed on the coffee table.

"Dinner?" It was Ronnie.

"Sure," I answered. It was the first communication we'd had since he'd left the hospital. "Where?"

"Bonefish," he replied, and I agreed to meet him at six thirty. Then I set the phone on the table and closed my eyes. I slept for an hour or so and then got ready to leave for dinner.

I had no idea what kind of evening to expect. I braced myself for a night of strained conversation and weird looks. Yes, Ronnie had asked me to dinner, but that didn't mean he wasn't going to be distant once he saw me and the memory of what we'd done was staring at him from across the table. Figuring I might as well get it over with, I got in my car and drove the few miles to the restaurant.

Ronnie was already there, and so were Jerry, Bobby, and Phillip. I approached the table and sat down, greeting everyone and ordering a drink when the server came to the table.

"How is your dad?" Jerry asked.

"Getting better all the time. There's still a chance the blockage could reform, but all we can do is deal with that if it happens." I put my napkin on my lap and glanced at Ronnie, who was deep in conversation with Bobby about some modification he wanted to make to one of his cars. It seemed like a waste to me, but Ronnie did what he wanted.

The server brought the drinks, and I sat quietly, listening and half wishing I was still back home. I figured I'd gotten Ronnie's message loud and clear. He'd chosen to ignore what happened altogether.

"That's great news about your dad," Ronnie said all of a sudden.

"Yeah, it is. Dad asked about you and said to thank you for coming down with me." I flashed him a quick smile. "It meant a lot to him and to me."

"You know I'd do anything for you, man," Ronnie said. "Family's important."

"It is." The server took our orders, and the dinner conversation denigrated to the usual topics centering around their various exploits—mostly Ronnie's—and the stupid things they'd all done.

"What's with you?" Phillip asked as he leaned close.

"What?" I mouthed.

The others were enthralled with one of Jerry's stories about the strangest places he ever had sex. Turned out this one was about an elevator.

"That elevator was either really slow, or you're a jackrabbit," Bobby ribbed. He earned a scowl from Jerry, who continued on with his story.

"You've been watching Ronnie all night," Phillip said quietly. "What's up with you? He's been looking at you strangely too. Did something happen?"

The others laughed. "No, everything is fine," I lied. "I'm just a little preoccupied with my dad and all." I resisted the urge to glance at Ronnie and lifted my glass as cover. I did my best to join in the main conversation, but by the time dinner was over, I was exhausted and I'd had enough. I had all the answer I thought I was going to get, so when the others got up to leave after paying the checks, I said good night and headed off to my car.

"Aren't you coming?" Bobby asked as he threw an arm over my shoulder. "Ronnie got a pool table and installed it in the basement. So we're going over to play." He steered me back to the group. I felt a bit like a wayward calf being driven back to the herd.

"I think I'm going to go home," I said weakly.

Ronnie had his phone pressed to his ear and seemed to be talking to a client. "Okay, great. Love you, man, talk to you soon." He hung up and shoved the phone in his pocket.

"Clay isn't coming to play pool with us," Bobby said like a tattletale four-year-old.

"Come on, Clay, don't be a pussy all your life," Ronnie teased. How many times had I heard that phrase during our friendship? It was classic Ronnie, and I began to think that things were going to be okay. He was acting normally. It was me who'd been strange, looking for a sign that wasn't there.

"For a while," I agreed against my better judgment.

"Can I get a ride with you?" Jerry asked.

"No problem." With the heat of the day gone, I put the top down on the convertible and put on my sunglasses before backing out of my space. The others were getting in their cars, and as we passed them, Jerry flipped them off. I rolled my eyes and kept my attention on the road while Jerry found a radio station he liked.

"This is a cool car," he yelled across to me as we sped up to enter the freeway.

"Thanks." I'd always loved it, and while my Mustang wasn't as eye-catching as one of Ronnie's exotics, I adored driving it.

"I want to get a new car, and there's a Porsche I have my eye on. It isn't new, but it would be cool," Jerry said.

"It would, but you remember how expensive Ronnie said they were to maintain?" I glanced over to catch a nod. Jerry had a decent job as an electrician, but he wasn't bringing in Porsche money, or even used-Porsche money.

"I was wondering what you think," he said.

"You were?" I was a little surprised. Jerry had never asked my advice before on anything.

"Yeah. You're the smart one in the group, and you don't do dumb things like the rest of us."

"If you want to know what I think, get a car you can truly afford. I bet your used Porsche costs as much as this car did new. You'll have problems with the used car because, well, it's used. Think about where you can get the most for your money and don't buy more car than you can afford. The last thing you want to do is get yourself into trouble over a car." I pulled off the exit and then to a stop at the end of the ramp. "Eventually you're going to want to get married, buy a house, and all the other things that come with having your own family. The last thing you want is something like a car deal that went wrong getting in the way of that. Your credit follows you forever." I could tell he wanted that car badly enough that he could taste it. He had that look in his eyes. "I know that isn't what you wanted to hear, but you aren't a kid anymore."

"My dad just got one, and—"

I pulled off the side of the road and motioned for him to come around. I walked to the passenger side and let him drive. "Your dad has worked his entire life. He raised you and your sisters. If he wants a fancy car, he deserves it. You need to think of your future, longer-term than the car you drive."

"That's what Dad says." Jerry pulled out and onto the road. "This is really nice. I like how it feels. The seat is really comfortable too."

"I really like it, and, Jerry, I can afford a Porsche if I want one. I make enough money that I could buy one. But then I wouldn't be able to go anywhere. No vacations, cruises, or nights out. It would be me sitting at home, looking at my Porsche." Come to think about it, that pretty much was my life already, minus the Porsche and going out with the guys a few times a week. "I know you want the car, but think about what you want for the future. You're twenty-seven, and I know you're dating a new girl."

"Yeah."

"And you really like her?" He blushed a little. "That much?"

"She's special, and I want to impress her."

Now things made sense. "A better way to impress her is to give her your attention. Show her she's special." We pulled to a stop. "Let me tell you something. Ronnie goes through girls like water because he gets their attention by what he has and spends, and it doesn't last. It doesn't matter what you drive. The girl for you will be impressed that you'd rather spend your time taking her to the movies or out to dinner, and listening to what she has to say, than by the car you're driving."

Jerry pulled into a parking space in Ronnie's development, and we got out. The others weren't there yet, so we waited outside. It didn't take long for Ronnie to pull right into his garage and come around to unlock the doors. Everyone filed down the stairs, and Bobby began setting up the table. I sat along the side, intent on watching. I let Jerry and Bobby play, and Phillip took on the winner, crowing when he won.

"What? You think because he's gay he can't be good at pool?" I asked Bobby and Jerry. "Have you forgotten we're good with balls?"

Jerry and Bobby groaned, and Phillip laughed and did a little shimmy dance while Ronnie clapped me on the shoulder.

"All right, let's you and me take on these two." Ronnie preened. "That is, if you're so good with balls."

I glared at him, inches from saying I was damned good with his and he knew it. "Fine." Jerry and Bobby won the break, so Bobby went, sinking one ball. Then it was Ronnie's turn, and he missed. Jerry sank one of the stripes.

"Come on, Clay, we're behind by two," Ronnie told me. "I'll let you suck my bird if you sink them all."

Of course we'd all heard that before. It was one of his standing jokes. "How about you suck me off?" I countered, cue in position.

"You sink them all, sure," Ronnie answered flippantly. I let the shot go and sank the first ball, then another. The cue ball seemed to land exactly where I wanted, and I took the third shot and then the fourth.

"I'm getting warmed up for you, babycakes," I whispered as I walked behind Ronnie. "It's going to be the experience of your life." I lined up the next shot and followed quickly with the sixth, and then the final solid ball dropped into the netted pocket. "Just the eight ball left."

"You have to call the pocket," Ronnie said with a slight tremor in his voice.

Of course I had no intention of having Ronnie make good on his moment of bravado, and the other guys knew it too, but it was funny to see the stiffness in Ronnie's usually unflappable posture.

"Side pocket." I made the shot, sinking the black ball, then grinned at Ronnie. "Do you want to do it here with an audience?" I hopped up on the side of the table and threw my head back, laughing as I spread my legs. The others laughed as well, and the tension that had momentarily filled the room burst like a bubble.

"Where did you learn to play like that?" Ronnie asked.

"In high school and college. I used to play all the time." There was something about the way the balls moved on the table that seemed to sing to me. It was geometry and physics in a confined space, and I loved it. "I haven't in a while, though."

"Can you run an entire table?" Jerry asked, setting his pool cue aside.

"I have a number of times. But no one can do it every time. That's the wonderful thing about this game. It's always different. I really got a little lucky this time." I handed my cue to Phillip so he could play and stepped back. Bobby pressed a beer into my hand and patted me on the shoulder as I took a seat and watched the others play.

"No," I told Jerry as he lined up a shot. "That's a sucker shot. It looks easy, but the angle is wrong. See, you have to lean all the way over the table, and the shot will be just far enough off that you'll miss. The shot here off the side and then into the pocket is a better bet. Aim for right here, and you'll be successful." Jerry looked dubious, but he took the shot and grinned when his ball dropped just as clean as could be. "Told you." Not to pick sides, I helped Phillip with his shot as well.

"That bet," Ronnie said.

"Don't worry about it. We were having fun." I met his gaze and lightly clinked my bottle to his. "I would never ask you to do something you didn't want."

Ronnie nodded slowly and drank from his bottle. We stood side by side, and I could feel the tension rolling off him in waves. What surprised me was that he didn't move away. It was like he wanted to ask me something, but wasn't sure how to say the words. "Is it always like—" He cut himself off and then cheered when Bobby dropped an amazing shot.

"No, Ronnie. It's rarely like that." I held his gaze for two seconds and then finished the last of my beer. I put my bottle with the others before going upstairs and getting another. I heard someone else on the stairs. Ronnie approached me, and I offered him another beer, but he shook his head. Ronnie didn't drink often. "You sure?" I didn't drink much myself, but I definitely wanted another.

"Cherie came back a few days ago."

I popped open the bottle and took a long drink. I really didn't want to hear this, but I couldn't stop myself. "What did she want?"

"To hop on the gravy train," he said. I nodded. "Of course she was all over me, and we...."

I rolled my eyes. "Yeah, I can imagine what you did."

"But it wasn't like.... She seemed.... I mean, I was like a machine, but...." He reached for my beer, and I handed him the bottle. "Things didn't work too well."

"Ronnie. She wasn't that interesting before." I shrugged and held back the smile I knew I shouldn't have.

"Yeah, I know. But there wasn't that...."

"Explosion at the end," I filled in for him, and he nodded. "Okay." I wasn't going to offer any advice. It was up to Ronnie at this point. I most certainly wasn't going to give him my view on what was wrong with that particular scenario.

"So what's wrong with me?" he asked. "I was fine with women until...."

I was so tempted to tell him that once tempted to the dark side, he couldn't go back, but I kept quiet. "Until what, Ronnie?" I grabbed another beer and leaned against the stainless-steel refrigerator door.

"Fuck you, Clay," he retorted, finishing the beer and then dropping the bottle in the recycling. "You know damn well what I'm talking about. Everything in my life was just fine until you—"

I growled and glared at him, hard as his granite counters.

"—until we," he corrected, "fucked while we were in Baltimore. Now it's all I think about, and going back to the way things were doesn't fucking work. So what in the hell do I do, screw around with guys now?"

I wanted to smack him so hard at that moment, I went so far as to lift my hand. I ended up clenching my hands into fists. "Have you ever had amazing, heart-stopping sex with women? I'm not talking adrenaline sex like the time you said you fucked in a cruise ship hot tub at night where anyone could see. I'm talking about amazing sex in your own bed, just from the person you were with?"

"Well, yeah."

"Okay, when?" I pressed. "Tell me about it." I tapped my foot on the floor. Because of all the sexual escapades Ronnie had ever talked about, they always involved wacky locations and girls who would do just about anything, but only after seeing the car he drove or one of his home-mortgage-expensive watches. I raised my eyebrows. "Not even with Maggie?" I asked him when he didn't answer me.

"I'm not a pig or something," Ronnie said.

Where did that come from? "I never said you were, or that there was anything wrong with you. But when we were together, you had a mind-blowing experience. Granted, it wasn't the way you've always seen yourself."

"You can say that again," Ronnie groaned.

"What do you want me to tell you, that I wish it hadn't happened?" I whispered. "Because I won't lie. It was as incredible for me as it was for you." I resisted the pull to step closer. The urge to just tell Ronnie how I felt was so close to the surface my tongue itched. But that would only scare him away. Patience was not one of my innate virtues. I'd had to learn it, and this situation required all I had.

"But I'm not gay," Ronnie said.

"Then fine. We'll forget about what happened. I'll never tell anyone." My chest tightened as I said the words, but what could I do? I wasn't going to pressure him into a relationship or anything he wasn't ready for, no matter how much I wanted to.

"But I can't," Ronnie whispered with desperation. "It's all I think about. Hell, it was what I was thinking about when I was with Cherie." In the time I'd known Ronnie, most of the time, with the exception of when he lost his dad, he was always bursting with confidence. He was the poster child for knowing who he was and being secure in himself. I had taken all that away from him. Why I couldn't have left well enough alone and just stayed away was beyond me. Ronnie was my friend, and I should have been content with that. He could have gone happily through his entire life without questioning himself like this.

"Then what do you want to do?" I asked. Ronnie shrugged. I heard footsteps on the stairs and left the kitchen, wandering into the small sitting area off the kitchen, staring out the windows that looked over the perfectly manicured lawn. I didn't want the others to see my expression until I had my emotions under some sort of control.

"Clay, it's your turn," Jerry called. "Phillip keeps winning so he wants to take you on."

"I'll be down in a minute," I answered and continued staring, but I wasn't seeing much. My thoughts occupied my attention. Then, after a few minutes, I turned and went downstairs, not really looking at the others.

I found Phillip grinning, with the rack set up and ready to go.

"You can break," I told him, and I let him get into position. He did very well, and the game was closer than any of the others had been. I won in the end but only by a few shots. Phillip saw it as a win, but I knew I was distracted and missed some shots I could have made if my heart had been in it. The others had wandered down and watched the last of the game.

I handed the cue to Jerry and sat down out of the way. The interest in pool was waning. They played another game, but they spent most of the time talking and goofing off rather than actually playing. "I think I'm going to head home," I told Ronnie in front of the others. It was getting late, and there was little need for me to stick around.

My pronouncement seemed to signal the end of the party, and the others all headed for the stairs as well. I took a few minutes to gather up some of the bottles and the small amount of trash, disposing of it before heading for the door. I found Ronnie in front of the garage. Bobby was giving Jerry a ride home, and they took off with a thrumming bass beat coming from the car. Phillip hurried over and gave both Ronnie and me a hug before racing off as well.

"I'll see you later." I wasn't sure if I should hug him or not and ended up with an awkward half handshake, half pat on the back. I shuffled out of the circle of light in front of the garage and went to my car. I sat back, letting the summer night air wash over me. I needed to breathe and think.

"Clay," Ronnie called as I was about to start the engine. I turned as he hurried over to where I was parked. "Pull your car in the drive."

"Ronnie...."

"Just do it," he snapped.

I could feel my stubbornness kick in, and I was seconds from digging in my heels and ignoring him. But then his hard expression shifted to nervous indecision, and I sighed, swearing under my breath, and did as he asked, parking the car in the light but not getting out. "What do you want, Ronnie?" I was way too tired for games. "If you want to talk, we can do that when we've both had a chance to think things over some more."

"Thinking is fucking overrated." He pulled open the car door, and I slowly got out. I wasn't sure how long I was going to be staying, but Ronnie climbed in and raised the top. Then he got out and motioned me inside the house, locking the door behind us.

I stood in the foyer, arms crossed over my chest, wondering what in the hell he wanted.

Ronnie strode past and grabbed my arm. The house was dark, and our footsteps echoed off the hardwood floors in the open space. Ronnie pulled open the bedroom door and gently tugged me inside. He didn't say a word. The bedroom door clicked closed, and he turned, staring at me in the light that came through one of the windows. I wanted to ask what he wanted, but I knew. I could read it in his questioning eyes and the way his lower lip disappeared every now and then. The message was loud and clear, delivered nervously in the slight sway as he changed his weight from foot to foot. Ronnie indecisive and nervous was a different man from the one I'd come to know and… yes, love, over the years.

Ronnie was a loudmouth who said anything that popped into his mind. But he also had the biggest heart of anyone I'd ever known. It just came in an unexpected package.

"What is it? Are you having trouble asking for what you want?"

"Yeah," he answered simply.

"All you have to do is say it."

He shrugged.

"It doesn't make you any less of a man or a person to be honest with yourself and ask for what you think you need." I stroked his cheek. "It takes strength to be different, the same courage it takes to ask for what's in your heart."

"You need me to say I want you to fuck me?"

"Is that all you really want?" I stepped closer, but he didn't answer. "All right, we'll take this slow. Go on into the bathroom and strip off for me, then start the water and get in the shower, nice and hot. I'll be there in just a minute." I kept my voice gentle and quiet. When he didn't move, I cupped his cheeks and drew him closer, kissing him.

"I don't need a shower," Ronnie said.

"Honey, this particular shower has very little to do with getting you clean. You'll understand." I waited as he turned and went toward the bathroom, looking back before stepping in. "Don't close the door," I added with a smile.

That appealed to his exhibitionist side, and he began pulling off his clothes while I rummaged in the bedside table and found what I was looking for. "Damn," I whispered when I turned around. Ronnie wore only a light pair of jeans and was about to unhook them at the waist. "Stop."

I walked over to him and brushed his hands away. Then, with only the very tips of my fingers, I traced over Ronnie's chest, around his nipples, and then down his chest to his hip bones. I slowly undid his jeans and let them slide down his beefy legs to the floor, seeing his cock jutting upward proudly.

He reached for it, but I stopped him. "Go start the water," I whispered, my mouth bone-dry. He turned, and I toed off my shoes and pulled my shirt over my head. He stepped into the shower, and I finished removing my clothes and got in behind him, grabbing the soap off the dish.

I lathered my hands well and slid them around his waist, running them up and down his chest. I stopped just above his cock, and he groaned more loudly each time his cock was denied. "Hey, we'll get to him in due time," I whispered, pressing him against the tile wall. Then I stroked down his back. "Spread your legs for me." He complied as I slid my hands over his ass. I tugged his hips back slightly and ran my soapy fingers along his crack. He tensed, and I stroked long and slow up his back.

"I'm going to fuck you until your brain melts, but I'm going to do it in the bed with you on your back, begging me to make you come." I sucked on one of his ears, and he tilted his head for better access. "That's it. Give yourself over to me for a while. I want you to concentrate on me and let the swirls of ideas and all that crap that runs through your head just fade away for now." I pushed my cock to his ass and ran my hands over his chest, lightly tweaking his nipples until he hissed softly.

The water poured over both of us, washing away the last of the soap. I pressed against Ronnie's back and began kissing his shoulder, then down his spine. The spray gushed down his body and over my head. I ignored it, kissing down the center of his back before licking and biting each of his asscheeks. "What are you doing?"

"Getting your attention," I told him, and then I spread his cheeks, teasing him with the tips of my fingers.

"You said not here," Ronnie said with a touch of anxiety.

I ran my tongue down his cleft and then over his tight little opening, and his initial gasp shifted to a groan that filled the small space. I licked him again, harder this time, teasing at his opening.

"Holy hell."

"Like that?" I asked.

Ronnie rested his arm and head on the tile, whimpering as I introduced him to the joys of rimming. His legs quivered like tentpoles in the wind. I probed and licked at Ronnie's muskiness, sucking small marks on his cheeks because, hell, I wanted him to be mine. The marks on his skin would fade soon enough, but I knew the bruises that would eventually be placed on my heart wouldn't fade nearly so quickly.

I slid a hand between Ronnie's legs, over his balls, and then along his cock, gripping him tightly. Tension built inside him until he was strung as tight as a drum. I wanted him that way, tight and excited under my hands. He was on the verge of coming—I could feel it. So I slowly began to stand, pulling my lips away, hands gliding back to my sides. I turned off the water, opened the shower door, and grabbed two towels. Ronnie moved in slow motion, blinking as though he'd just awakened from a dream.

He dried himself mechanically, his attention on whatever was running through his head. I dried off as well and then followed him out of the shower. He wandered into the bedroom, and I threw the towels over the shower door before turning off the light and following him.

Ronnie lay back on the bed, turned toward me, his gaze following every move I made. The room was mostly dark, with some light coming in through the windows from the neighbor's outside lighting.

"What are you thinking about?" I asked as I climbed on the bed.

"The appointments I have on Monday," he answered honestly. I knew he'd slipped away from me—I could see it in his eyes.

I ran my hands up his thighs, spreading his legs a little farther apart. "Are you thinking about business meetings now?" I asked and then blew my breath over his cock, setting it to jumping slightly. "Or are you thinking about how good my mouth is going to feel as I try to suck your brains out through your dick?" I licked the dark head, sucking it between my lips and then letting it go. "What are you thinking about now?"

"You," he said shakily.

"Yeah. That's what I want. You just think about me for a while." I sucked him in once again, sliding my tongue over him. He shook as I took him all the way, my nose buried in his skin, inhaling the increasingly aroused scent of him.

I came up for air, inhaled, and then swallowed him once again.

"Jesus Christ, how can you do that?"

I grinned when I let him slip from my lips and slowly moved to straddle his hips.

"Do you want me to fuck you?" he asked.

"No," I told him, leaning forward to capture his lips. "But will you suck me?" As soon as I said it, I knew it was too much. He stilled, and I backed away, sucking on a nipple and then moving backward. By the time I had sucked him deep once again, Ronnie was groaning and writhing on the bedding. "You have a great cock," I told him.

"I always told you I had a good bird," Ronnie said.

"Yeah." I pressed a finger beside his cock, getting it wet before slowly entering him. "And you know just what I can do with my cock." He shook when I pressed against his gland. "Just think about it. I can make you come with just my cock."

"You mean no hands?" he asked.

"Oh yeah." I kissed the center of his chest and then captured his lips, kissing him hard, taking possession of his mouth while I slowly rubbed inside him, sending ripples of passion through him again and again. "I can make you come without touching you."

"How?" Ronnie challenged.

I withdrew my finger and reached to the nightstand. I got the slick and coated two fingers. By the time I had them embedded inside him, scissoring them and touching him just right every now and then, Ronnie was gasping for breath, eyes wide, cock bouncing on his belly.

I got a condom and rolled it on my cock, slicked it up, and then slowly entered him, holding his legs. "I want you to put your arms over your head."

"Why?"

"Because this is going to be intense, and you're going to want to touch yourself because I'm going to hold you on the edge as long as I can. Everything inside you is going to scream that you want to come, but it's too soon. You have to trust that when I do make you come, it will all be worth it."

I sank deeper, slowly filling him, his body clutching my cock in a death grip. Tight didn't begin to describe how he felt, and as hard as he gripped my cock, I could feel Ronnie taking hold of my heart. It was way too soon for that, but I felt it anyway. I couldn't stop it no matter how I tried, so I let it happen, the consequences be damned.

I pressed my hips to his ass, gave him a few seconds to breathe, and then slowly pulled away. I lifted my hips up just enough that he gasped, and then I slid my cock at just the right angle.

"Fuck!"

"Yeah, I know, and I can stay right there." I sank deep inside him, and Ronnie's mouth hung open. "Can you feel it already?"

Ronnie nodded.

"You talk all the time—you never shut up, so you can speak now. You have to tell me."

"I...."

"Let me guess. Your dick is going to explode. You're as hard as you can ever remember feeling in your life." I leaned forward,

79

snapping my hips just a little, sucking on Ronnie's ear. "You want to come so bad your eyes are crossing and air seems impossible to pull into your lungs." He whimpered and nodded. "You never want this to end, but know it will as soon as you come, so you're holding it back with everything you have."

"Jesus...," he groaned under his breath.

"Yeah, but you can't. The control you crave is slipping away from you by the second. Every time my cock touches you inside, you get closer and closer." I sucked his ear once again as the quivering shakes tore through him. I knew that when someone was in the zone the way I had him, it didn't matter if what I told him was true. Just saying the words could make it true.

"I need...." Ronnie lifted his arms, and I grasped his wrists.

"Not yet. I know you're so close. Coming is all you can think about, but not yet." I stilled, pressing deep inside him, my cock throbbing with my impending release. My heart pounded in my ears, and it would've been so easy to thrust fast, to let my instincts take over and carry us both away. But that wasn't the purpose. I needed to bring Ronnie with me and let him know I could play him like a symphony.

"When?" he begged.

"Soon, once the tingling in your balls spreads to your back and then zings up your spine, settling at the base of your brain, humming there, waiting to explode into a ball of erotic fire that will engulf you."

"Yeah...." Ronnie whimpered. "Jesus, I...."

"I'll hold you and keep you from flying apart. You need to hold on for me, just a few more seconds." I kissed him hard, and he gave back to me, adding his own energy. That was what I'd been waiting for: the moment Ronnie gave himself to me completely. There was no hesitation, and I thrust faster, adjusting the angle until his moans grew frantic and filled with the last vestiges of control.

"I can't... I'm gonna...."

"I know. Clench yourself, pull me over with you!" Ronnie clenched his muscles, his body like a vise around my cock. "That's it, baby, now come for me. Let go and soar!"

"God, I'm—" He screamed at the top of his lungs, every muscle clenching. I tumbled over the edge as Ronnie came.

"That's it. Let it go. Let it all go." I balanced on the very edges of control. I had to remain present as Ronnie lost it, coming under me in shouts that morphed into a cry and ended in near agony. I saw tears slide down Ronnie's cheeks and pretended not to. That I could pull that kind of emotion from him was enough. He didn't need to know that I saw it happen.

Our bodies separated, and I shifted to lie on the bed next to him, pulling him to me. I managed to get the condom off and put it on a tissue, and then I held Ronnie while he quivered next to me. I wasn't sure what I'd released, but Ronnie's shoulders shook, and I knew he was crying. Somehow I'd unlocked some part of him that had been held so closely for so long, and now it was out.

He didn't say anything, even after whatever storm I'd released had passed and he settled quietly on the bed.

"Are you all right?" I whispered, gently kissing his shoulder.

"I don't know."

"All right. You know that's okay. None of us has to have the answers all the time, even about ourselves." I stroked his belly, making slow, lazy circles with my hand, spreading and rubbing his release into his warm skin.

"That's kind of weird."

"No, it's not. We spend all our time in our own heads, and sometimes we're too close. We can't deal with things, so we lock them away, and then they come pouring out when we don't expect it." I pulled him tighter. "Do you want to tell me what happened?"

Ronnie shuddered. "No," he replied in a half gasp, and his belly fluttered. I knew he was close to tears once again, and that scared the hell out of me. I had never seen Ronnie cry other than for his dad. This was different. This was a cry not of loss, but of inner anguish.

"I have you. Just let it out. Whatever it is, you can deal with it." I felt tears prickle my own eyes, and I had no idea why, other than I was sharing whatever pain Ronnie was experiencing.

"I can't."

"Yes, you can. If you don't want to tell me, you don't have to. But I'm here and I won't let you go." I lightly smacked his hip.

"What was that for?"

"Whatever we released can't be put back in the bottle. So don't try. It's out there. You're a strong man, and you can deal with anything." I wanted to get something to clean him up, but I wasn't going to let go of him for even a second. He needed to know that I was right there for him, and that I would stay that way.

"I…. This has nothing to do with you. But I can't…." Ronnie started to shake again, and I gently rubbed his hip and side. "How could I have forgotten this?" he groaned under his breath. I didn't think he meant for me to hear it, and I pretended I didn't. Some things were private, and paramount among those were our own thoughts.

"You don't have to talk about it." I closed my eyes and lay still. I was tired, and fatigue was catching up with me. "But try to rest."

"I won't, not with this hanging over me," Ronnie whispered.

I shifted back and rolled him over to face me. "Yes, you can. I know your mind goes in circles, but this isn't something you can deal with right now. So I want you to close your eyes and let it go. I need you to think of something else." I leaned closer. I stroked his cheek. "Concentrate on me and how I made you feel. I just blew your mind, and I want you to remember how your heart pounded and how your entire body ached for my touch. Close your eyes and think of nothing other than that."

"How?"

"In the winter when you get cold, you wrap yourself in a warm blanket. Let the memories of what we just did be that blanket for you." I got out of the bed, and Ronnie grabbed my arm, our gazes locking. "I'm not leaving you." He let go, and I hurried to the luxurious bathroom and grabbed a washcloth, placed it under warm water, and then got a towel and returned to the bedroom. Ronnie sat up, the bedding draping over his legs and waist. I handed him the cloth, and he pushed the bedding away and washed himself. Then he held it out so I could take it. "Don't get used to this kind of service all the time."

Ronnie took on an imperious air, and I snatched the cloth and towel from him, tossing them through the bathroom door. "Why did you do that?" he asked.

I climbed on the bed. "I am not one of your Silicone Sues, and I'm not a servant either. I did what I did to be nice." I shifted closer to him. "You might get the bimbos you usually fuck to act like slaves, but I won't."

"What do you want, then?"

"How about a thank-you when I do something for you rather than you acting as though it's your due," I chastised. "I'm a man, the same as you." I glared at him. "Now lie back down and go to sleep." I thought he was going to fight me on it, but he reclined, watching me, and I settled under the covers.

Ronnie turned over multiple times. "It's not working."

"Do you want me to go?" I figured I might be unnerving him.

"No," he answered quickly.

"All right." I propped my head on my hand and then gave up. I was too tired, and that position hurt my neck. I ended up pulling Ronnie to me, spooning against his back, and he squirmed. I smacked his ass lightly. "If my dick on your ass bothers you, it's a little late now." He settled on the bed, but I knew he was just lying there. "Tell me what it's like," I said.

"What?" he asked huffily.

"In your head. What are you thinking about right now?"

"I keep playing what happened over and over again. It's like a movie that won't shut off. When my dad died I kept seeing him, and then the grief of his loss would return again and again. I'd think I was getting past it, but it would play on continuous loop, and I would feel just as bad as I did before the funeral." Ronnie paused. "Now I'm at his funeral again. I had to get up and talk to everyone because my mother couldn't do it. I'm standing there, and I can see everyone looking at me, faces sad, expecting me to say something to make it all better, and I can't."

"All right." His agitation was palpable. "I want you to roll onto your stomach." I climbed off the bed. "Just lie there and put your arms out to your sides. I'll be right back, and I want you to concentrate on breathing. In through your nose and out through your mouth."

"Clay…," he groused.

"If you don't, when I get back, I'll smack your ass until it's red and burning. That will take your mind off what's rolling around in it, but I have a much better way—one I know you're going to like. So just breathe and think about that." I went into the bathroom and rummaged in the medicine cabinet. The damn thing was full of prescription bottles. "Shit." I wondered what all that crap was for. I eventually found some hand lotion. It was clean smelling and not overpowering. I grabbed it and turned off the light as I left the room.

After setting the bottle on the nightstand, I tugged the curtains fully closed to cut off as much spillover light as possible and even shut down the computer and turned the clock to the wall to quell the light. Then I climbed back on the bed, feeling my way to the lotion. It had never occurred to me just how splintered Ronnie was on the inside. He put up a good front, but that kind of thinking was going to drive him crazy. No wonder he did all the things he did—the wild purchases and the impulsive behavior.

I squirted some lotion onto my hands and started at his shoulders. "Be sure to tell me what you like," I told him quietly, stroking firmly down his back. "Remember to breathe." I nestled my cock, which had awakened and taken a keen interest in what was going on, against Ronnie's ass and continued the massage. Up his back and over his shoulders, then gently up and around his neck before sliding down the center of his back and along his sides. I continued until I felt the tension begin to lessen.

"God, that's good," Ronnie breathed.

"Good." I shifted down his legs and worked my hands over his hard ass. Kneading his cheeks, I got more lotion and worked the skin. "Like that?"

"Yeah." He drew the word out, long and slow.

I shifted off his legs and gently spread them. "Lift your hips."

"Huh," he whimpered as I guided his hips upward.

"That's it, spread your legs," I whispered, massaging his butt. I added more lotion and then slid my hands down his quivering thighs before reversing and gently cupping his balls.

"Oh God, that's…."

I slid my hand along his cock, encircling the hard shaft and stroking it slowly.

"I know." I pulled my hands back up to his balls and then over his ass. He shook on the bed as I teased his opening without entering. I didn't want him sore, just relaxed, so I kept moving my hands, sliding them over his balls and then up his cock. Ronnie moaned softly as I continued stroking him.

Ronnie rocked back and forth, and when I slowly breached him with a finger, I found his gland, and his groans reached a fever pitch. I knew he was ready to come, and I drove him over the edge. Then I pulled my hand away, rubbing his back to soothe him as he came back down.

"I think I need that towel again," Ronnie said, and I got him one. He cleaned up the bedding and then climbed back under the covers, sighing and still breathing heavily. "Thank you."

"Just go to sleep," I whispered and got him to roll over. Within minutes he was asleep, breathing slowly and deeply, even as my mind started running through possible scenarios. Unfortunately, many of them ended badly.

CHAPTER 5

I WOKE in Ronnie's bed. He was still asleep, and when I rolled to the edge of the bed, Ronnie rolled over but didn't wake. He seemed happy and relaxed, which was good. I got out of the bed and grabbed my clothes, then went into the bathroom and dressed. I hadn't been planning to stay, so I put on what I had and quietly left the bedroom. I went right into the kitchen and found the coffee, then got a pot brewing. I also looked in the refrigerator to see if there was anything in it. Of course it was just as empty as ever, with the exception of protein drinks.

I gave up and poured a mug of coffee when it was ready, retrieved the paper from outside the door, and settled in to read.

"I was wondering where you were," Ronnie said when he wandered out of the bedroom, naked. "Is that coffee?"

"Yes. I made a pot. Go get dressed, and you can have a cup. I tried to find something for breakfast, but the place is devoid of food."

"We'll meet the guys before going to the gym," Ronnie said after yawning.

"I need to go home," I explained.

"Why?"

"I don't have any fresh clothes. All the guys will wonder why I'm wearing the same clothes as yesterday, so unless you're prepared to answer questions about what happened last night, and why I stayed with you, I need to get home and change."

Ronnie nodded. "I'll message the guys, and we'll meet for breakfast in an hour." I handed him his coffee and watched his perky bare ass as he walked back to the bedroom. I finished my mug, placed the dish in the sink, and then walked to the front door. I left the house and got in my car, pointing it toward home.

I parked in front of my house and hurried inside. I didn't need to shower, but I did clean up and shave quickly, and changed clothes. I also packed my gym bag. Ronnie sent a text that said to meet for breakfast in ten minutes, so I headed to Panera.

Ronnie and the others were already there, in the heat of an intense conversation. I joined them and found a bagel and cream cheese waiting for me. "Thanks," I told Ronnie, who nodded. I started eating and noticed that Ronnie grew quiet. The other guys talked, but he sat and listened.

"What's up with him?" Phillip asked me when Ronnie got up for more iced tea.

I shook my head. I figured it had to do with what had upset him the night before, but I didn't know any of the details, and I didn't want to have to explain. "Just give him some space if he needs it," I told him. Phillip shrugged and turned his attention to the conversation.

"You okay?" I asked Ronnie when he sat back down.

"Yeah," he answered, but I knew it was a lie. It was written on his face.

I ate quickly, then got up to refill my glass. When I returned they were still talking about God knows what. "Hey, guys, let's head on over," I prompted. Ronnie needed something to occupy his mind, and exercise would work well for him. It usually did.

Ronnie stood and seemed to click back to the present. "Let's get Johnny Beefcake." Whatever the hell that meant, but it was the first sign of his usual energy I'd seen all morning. The guys talked their way out of the restaurant and to the cars.

It was like a convoy as we all drove to the gym. I brought up the rear and followed the others inside before heading up to the cardio equipment. Ronnie and the rest of the guys went to the weights. I watched them, and Ronnie seemed more his normal self. He talked with everyone, telling stories and shooting his mouth off the way he always did. But even from where I was, I could see it was forced. His body was stiffer than usual, and he kept looking around, watching the others. It was very strange, like his outward veneer was in place, but underneath, his world had been rocked to the core, and it showed in everything he did.

I tried not to worry. I opened the book I'd brought with me to pass the treadmill time, but I couldn't concentrate on a single word.

"Hey, big guy."

I turned as Michael, a friend from work, got on the treadmill next to me. "Hey, Michael. How are you doing? I haven't seen you in a while. What have they had you up to? How's the European office treating you?" I smiled after my barrage of questions.

"Really well. I'm going to be staying for quite a while," he said. "I really like it there. But with some of the projects going on right now, they've asked me to be the interface for the organization there, so I'll be doing some traveling back and forth."

"Did Stephan come over with you?" I asked, happy to take my mind off the whole Ronnie situation for a few minutes. Michael's partner, Stephan, was based in the Netherlands.

"No. He's still got to work, but next time I think he'll come over, and we'll tack on some vacation time here in the States. Although we've had some amazing vacations in the last few years—Italy, Spain, Malta, South Africa. All these exotic places are so easily accessible from Amsterdam." He started his machine, and I waited for him to get up to speed. "How are things here?"

"All right," I said. Michael and I had been friends for years and fairly close until he took the assignment in the Netherlands a few years ago. Not that I could blame him, when he'd found the love of his life over there. "I'm single again."

"When did that happen?" He seemed surprised.

"Two years ago. Brian decided he didn't love me any longer. Personally I think he was looking for a younger model, and if the rumors are true, he found one." I sighed and smacked myself inwardly for even bringing it up.

"Are you over it?" Michael asked.

"Yeah, I really think I am." My reaction surprised me, and it felt good. "He's entitled to his life and what makes him happy. If that's a collection of twinks, so be it." I shrugged.

"Then if you don't mind my asking, why the long face? When I came up, you looked like you were trying to solve world hunger. Not that it's any of my business," he added quickly.

"It's okay. I started something I'm not sure I should have." I shifted my gaze to Ronnie, and Michael followed it.

"You've got to be kidding me. He's straight. He was married, right? And hasn't he been dating that girl, ummm, Maggie, for a long time?" Michael must have known Ronnie from before he left for the Netherlands. Sometimes it still amazed me how everyone seemed to know Ronnie.

"They broke up," I told him. "Anyway, to make a long story short, he isn't as straight as I thought... or he thought, as a matter of fact."

"Are you dating?" Michael asked.

I shook my head. "We're fucking but nothing more than that right now." I sighed. "I know you'll keep that to yourself." Michael nodded and mimed buttoning his lip. "Have you ever wished you'd kept the genie in the bottle?"

Michael took a drink from his water bottle. "What do you mean?"

"Like I said, he isn't as straight as he thought he was, but I'm willing to bet he would have gone through the rest of his life happily dating women. He would have been 'normal' for most people and happy in his ignorance." I hoped to hell I was explaining this right. "Now that I... introduced him to the gay side...." I tilted my head. "You knew Ronnie before you left. Have you ever seen him sit on a bench deep in thought?"

"God, no," Michael said. "He's usually out there talking to everyone."

"Exactly."

"And this is your fault, how? Did you force yourself on him?"

I lost my footing and nearly flew off the back of the machine. I managed to catch myself and regain my stride. "Of course not. But it started off as sort of a joke and then got serious pretty fast. He never would have suggested...." I tried to put my rambling thoughts together and failed. "I figured I'd tease him and he'd laugh it off, but he didn't, and then we were together."

"And you think you're responsible for his internal debate?" Michael shook his head. "Maybe he would have been better off in his ignorance, but if he has feelings for other men, they were going to come out sooner or later, and maybe with someone who doesn't care as much about him as you obviously do." Michael grinned. "Does it really matter if you let him fuck you? I mean, a lot of straight guys are horny enough to—"

I shook my head slowly. "That's not what I meant."

Michael thought for a minute and then inhaled sharply. "You mean you... and he...." His mouth dropped open. "My God."

"He's amazing," I told him. "But that's beside the point. He was trying to comfort me while my dad was sick, and then I was trying to help him, and—"

Michael laughed. "Bullshit. That had nothing to do with you. A straight guy is not going to comfort anyone with butt sex," he whispered. "No way, no how. And if you want my opinion, you're blaming yourself for things you shouldn't. If he is having some sort of identity crisis, then you need to be there for him and help him through it. But don't blame yourself for it."

I blew air out of my lungs. "That's easy for you to say."

"Sexual identity isn't black-and-white. We'd all like to think it is—even gay people. It's easier to put everyone in a box and keep them there. But it doesn't work that way. You and I are gay so that makes things easier. He's obviously some form of bisexual or even pansexual."

"Yeah, it seems he likes everyone," I joked.

"Maybe. Or he's bisexual and prefers women except when it comes to you," Michael suggested. "I don't know, and neither do you. But if you're willing to put in the effort, you might find out."

Michael was a great guy, and I suddenly realized how much I'd missed him. We used to go to dinner sometimes, and we'd always been good friends at the office. There weren't that many gay people where we worked, so we all knew each other.

"I feel bad for bringing all this into his life. If I'd left well enough alone and kept my hands to myself, none of this would be happening."

Michael smirked at me. "For God's sake, get down off the cross—someone else needs the wood." He grinned widely. "I always wanted to be able to use that."

"Smartass," I retorted.

"Well, Christ on the cross didn't groan as much as you are. Give it a rest. You aren't responsible for the whole world, just you. And you didn't do anything to Ronnie that he didn't agree to."

"But...."

"All you can do is help him through this," Michael said.

"But what if he... what if he decides to go back to the way things were?" I asked, finally able to give voice to what was really bothering me.

"That's the crux of it, isn't it? You're worried he'll decide he doesn't want you and will go back to dating women again. And he might. Again, that's out of your control."

"You're just a ray of sunshine, aren't you?" I retorted with a sigh. "I know you're right." I turned back to look at Ronnie. "I just...."

"The real problem is that you're in love with him," Michael said. "You can hide it or try to tell yourself that you aren't, but that's what's happened." He pressed Pause on the treadmill. "It's written all over your face, bud. I can see it, and so can anyone else who's looking for it."

"What the hell do I do?"

"Help him. Be there for him, and if he isn't ready to go where you want him to, grieve alone and in private unless you want to lose him as a friend."

"Shit," I breathed as Michael restarted his treadmill. I was so screwed.

THE REST of the workout was next to useless. All I did was watch and worry over Ronnie. I didn't have a chance to get him alone to talk to him, so all I could do was wonder. In the sauna after working out, he at least seemed up to his normal storytelling, so I sat back and hoped to hell the heat sweated out my concern. Of course it didn't help much, and after rinsing off, I used the whirlpool and then went into the showers.

Ronnie and the guys played their usual games, snapping towels to see who could leave the biggest marks on whose backside. I swear, get any four guys together and they instantly reverted to the age of the youngest guy minus a decade. I stayed out of the line of fire, cleaned up, and left to get dressed.

The guys were making plans to go to lunch, but I didn't feel up to it. I was tired and needed some alone time. I walked with the guys out to the front and said good-bye.

"You aren't coming?" Ronnie asked. "It's Thai food, your favorite."

"I'm going to go home and get some things done. Have fun at lunch, and I'll call you later." I forced a smile and walked out to my car. Maybe a little distance between me and Ronnie would help me get some perspective. I threw my bag in the trunk, lowered the top on the car, and slowly drove the mile or so home.

I should have known that sitting home alone with my thoughts, eating a ham sandwich because it was all the food I had in the house, wouldn't make me feel better. I ended up throwing part of it away and banging the back door as I went outside to putter in the yard. Working out or gardening usually helped me work through whatever problem I had. The former hadn't done anything, so I tried the latter. It didn't really work very well either, but I did get the last bed in the yard cleared of weeds and mulched.

My phone chimed with a message. It was Ronnie.

Where are you?

At home in the garden, working, I answered and set my phone aside.

Why?

That was not the response I expected.

I need to get some things caught up because I was gone.

I can think of a million things more fun to do than that. I'd rather put my nuts in a vise than do yard work.

At least his raunchy sense of humor was returning.

I like it.

I figured that was the end of the exchange, set my phone in the grass, and returned to my work. It remained silent, and I continued edging the bed.

"So, Captain Cock, what in the hell are you doing?"

I set my tool aside. "What are you doing here?" I asked as Ronnie strode across my lawn. "I figured you'd still be at lunch, talking."

"Nope. Jerry had to be somewhere, and Bobby said he had to visit his mother. Phillip begged off, probably to smoke some pole somewhere."

"You really can be an ass," I told him.

"It's part of my charm." At least the bravado was back.

"So you worked through what was bothering you?" I asked.

"No. And thanks for bringing it up so I can stew on it some more." He grabbed one of the chairs and sat down, turning it so he could watch me. "Yard work is fascinating. I could watch you do it all day."

"Ha-ha," I responded and began gathering up my tools. There was no use working any longer. Ronnie obviously wanted something, and he intended to take his time getting around to it. "I'll get some tea. Be right back." I hurried inside and filled my jug with cold water and tea bags. I should have done it earlier, but what the hell. I closed the lid and set the jug in the sun.

"A little slow, isn't it?" Ronnie asked as he watched the tea bags float on the water.

"I could brew the tea or use some instant stuff I have in the cupboard." I wasn't disappointed when Ronnie screwed up his face in distaste. "It doesn't take that long. So what did you stop by for?"

"You should have come to lunch with the rest of us," Ronnie said gruffly. "You can't sit here all the time, alone, up to your elbows in dirt."

"I wasn't, and I like gardening." But I thought I knew what Ronnie was saying. I hadn't always gone to lunch after we went to the gym on weekends, and he'd never stopped by my house afterward before. "I think you're going to have to try better than that."

"What the hell does that mean?"

I wasn't going to let him off the hook. "Just say what you want to say."

"What? That I missed you at lunch?" Ronnie stood, glaring at me. "Okay, I did, and I was pissed that you just took off after the gym."

"Okay. But is it so bad that I needed a chance to think?"

Ronnie walked across the patio to the bed where the peonies were just starting to fade but still looked radiant. He stared at the flowers, his back to me for a full two minutes. "You aren't the one whose entire outlook got kicked in the nuts." He whirled to face me. "But you're the one who needs to think," he added sarcastically.

"I figured I'd give us both time to think."

Ronnie stormed over to my chair and placed his hands on the arms, his face inches from mine. "All I ever do is fucking think. My mind never shuts the hell off. It goes round and round in circles all the fucking time, and I run the same things over and over because I'm afraid of forgetting something. Does that sound like someone who needs more time to fucking think?"

My mouth dropped open in surprise. "I thought with the things you'd... that we'd done, you'd need some time to figure shit out. I know I do."

"Why?" Ronnie demanded. "You know who the hell you are. You always have." He chuckled. "Shit, I knew you were gay and proud of it the first time I saw you in the gym wearing the smallest shorts known to man and that string tank that showed off your little pink nipples. You couldn't have been more gay, and you didn't care who knew or what anyone thought. I liked you for that. Why do you think I started talking to you?" He pushed himself back and strode onto the grass. "I always thought I knew who I was too."

"And who's that?"

94

"I'd reach the pinnacle of my job, which I nearly have. I'd find a woman who was gorgeous and hot as hell, and in the bedroom she'd be a freaky whore who couldn't get enough. And I nearly had all of it. Then my dad died, Maggie left, and my world fell apart." The anguish in his voice tore at my heart.

"I know all that," I said softly.

"Last night, it all started again. I couldn't make any of it stop, and then…." He paused and glanced around.

"Just say what you want to say. There's nothing to be ashamed of," I told him gently.

"Fine. You fucked the shit out of me and brought back stuff I thought was a nightmare. But it wasn't." His hands shook. "It happened when I was a kid, and I need to talk to my mom. But the thing is, while we were having sex, both times, my mind was silent. The wheels stopped, and my head was clear. That's never happened before. After the second time, I couldn't think at all. I lay in bed, and for the first time I can ever remember without being on drugs that made me high as a kite, my mind was clear and settled."

I was shocked and tried to speak. My lips moved but nothing came out right. Finally, I said, "I don't understand. I think I know what you're saying, but… how? And it never happened with anyone else?"

"No. Maggie was a freak in bed. She wanted it as much as me, but half the time I was fucking her and my head was swirling with customer appointments or the shit with my dad. Once, when my mom was in the hospital, I fucked Maggie while worrying if Mom was okay. It's freaky crazy, but that's how my head works. Until you."

"So that's good?"

"Yeah, but I'm not gay," he whispered, almost like a prayer.

"No, you're not. You're bisexual," I told him. "You're one of those guys who loves sex, and it seems you like both men and women."

"But I didn't need to know that. I could have been happy with women," he snarled.

Now it was my turn to get agitated, and I pushed him back so I could get up. I was starting to feel trapped in that chair, especially when he pressed closer to me. "Don't you think I know that? Why do you think I didn't go to lunch? If nothing had happened between us, you would have been blissfully unaware and could have gone on with your life." I cringed inwardly, and I strode across the yard before turning back to him. "You still can. Just forget what happened between us and return to the life you had before." The thought ripped at my heart, and I had to turn away so he didn't see my expression. If he did, I'd never be able to get the words out. "We can still be friends, and I'll never speak about any of this. You can go back to meeting women and try to find someone you see yourself spending the rest of your life with. You deserve to be happy." There was no fucking way I was going to stand in his way. I cared too much about him to do that. Fucking hell—I was in love with him. Michael was right. I'd loved him for a long time as a friend, but my feelings had intensified so quickly they had my head spinning. That was the only explanation for the burning so deep in my chest I could barely breathe. I should have seen this coming.

"If that's what you want," Ronnie said.

"What I want has nothing to do with it, you moron. It's what you want. That's what counts, and you need to figure out what the hell that is." Now that I had my rampant emotions under tenuous control, at least for now, I turned to Ronnie. What I saw startled me. I wanted to smack that "I want to have my cake and eat it too" look off his face. I knew it well, because he always thought there was a way for him to have it all.

"It's just sex," Ronnie said.

I shook my head. "I fucking knew it," I ground out. "You figure you can date some chick and then whenever you want, we can—" I stepped closer. "I'm not the male version of one of your Silicone Sues. And I will not be your sex toy to haul out whenever you're feeling randy or need your head wheels stopped or whatever other stupid idea you have running in that fucking skull of yours. I won't be a dirty little secret."

"But you said you wouldn't tell anyone," Ronnie said.

"And I meant it. But you have to decide what you want. And just so we're clear, me being your fuck buddy on the side is not an option. See, I've noticed something. I keep saying that I want you to be happy, but you've never said anything like that to me. You were trying to figure out how you could get what you wanted… and that's all." I turned away and kicked at a dandelion head in my otherwise nearly perfect lawn. "For you it was just sex, but it wasn't that for me. It was more than sex."

"So you want a life with me… together…." His voice made it clear that the idea was as foreign to him as licking a skunk's ass. "Isn't that—"

I cut him off. "I'm just saying that you have some thinking to do. You were the one who said you could have been happy in your ignorance, but you know things about yourself now, and I'll be here as best I can for you. But remember I'm a person too." God, I didn't know what the hell I was trying to say. I should've just walked away and let him go on with his life. "You don't owe me anything, Ronnie. We had sex, and if that's all it was, then that's fine." I took a deep breath and wondered when I'd turned so clingy.

"Do you want me to go?" he asked.

"You don't have to." It probably would be better if he did. "Go ahead and sit down and relax. It's quiet here and the breeze is really nice." I took the other chair and closed my eyes.

"Are all gay guys as weird as you?" Ronnie asked with a touch of amusement.

"Now that's the pot calling the kettle black," I said, smiling.

"I'm not weird."

"Please. You certainly are. You live in a grand place with a kitchen anyone would die to have, and nothing is ever used. And for goodness sake, don't get me started on your taste in furniture. Who was your decorator, Edgar Allan Poe?"

"I decorated my place, and I have great taste."

"No, you don't."

"Excuse me?" he said.

"What don't you understand about no? It's an easy concept. Maybe I'll say it slower. Noooooooooo." I was happy the conversation had lightened up somewhat. "I like the bedroom, but the rest of it is too weird for words."

"See? You are weird. My place is happening."

"Ask your mom," I told him. "The next time you talk to Dolores, ask her. She's an artist and she'll tell you. You think you have great taste, but it's all born of impulses. And you know it. Like the baseball cards the other day. You get upset and buy stuff. Sometimes really cool stuff," I added with a shrug. "Does that go back to the turning wheels in your head?"

I expected him to get defensive. "I think so, and I didn't buy the cards."

"That's good. You know I'm your friend, and you hate to hear that you're wrong from anyone, but sometimes you aren't doing yourself any favors." How we'd gotten onto this topic I wasn't sure. "You don't need the latest shiny gadget or the biggest and baddest car to show everyone who you are. Being Ronnie is good enough. You're good enough."

"I know that," he said really quickly.

"I just wanted you to know that without the cars and the watches and everything else you have, I'd still be your friend and like you for you. The things that make you special aren't on the outside and aren't what you drive or have. They're who you are on the inside, and that's why when you came over that day we first met, I wanted to be friends with you and get to know you. Ronnie, you have this way of adding light to a room and making people laugh. That's your real talent and why you're successful. Everything else is set dressing." I closed my eyes to cut off the connection between us for a few seconds. I was dangerously close to revealing my true feelings, and I was sure that would spell disaster.

"I'm glad you think I'm so status-obsessed," Ronnie said angrily.

"That's what you got out of what I said?" I shook my head. "I meant that all the cars and stuff aren't important to me or any of your friends. You don't need to impress us—we already like you."

He stood, and I did the same.

"I better go." Ronnie turned and strode out the gate to his car. I stayed where I was, believing that our friendship and everything else was most likely over. His stiff posture screamed that he'd heard more than he could comprehend and was going into defensive mode.

Ronnie never walked away without saying that he'd text or call. At the very least he'd ask me to. But today he said nothing, and I watched as he got in his car. The engine roared to life, and then the tires screamed as he took off. Once he was out of sight, I thought about going back to work, but my heart wasn't in it. I put the tools away and gathered everything up before going inside and curling on the sofa to watch television.

The phone rang a few minutes later. "Hey, Dad," I said when I answered. "How's it going?"

"Not bad," he said, sounding tired. "They're making me exercise some, and I can't eat what I want."

"You had a stroke. They need to get the blood flowing and make sure there aren't any more blockages."

"When are you coming back to see me?"

"Next weekend. I have to work this week, but I'll come down on Friday and go home on Saturday. Have they said how long they expect you to stay?"

"A few more weeks, I guess. If I had someone at home, I could probably go home earlier, but they said they want me to be strong enough to take care of myself, and I can't argue with that."

"True."

"How are you?" he asked. "Have you seen your friend who came down with you? He was real nice. Tell him I appreciate his being here. I'm glad you weren't alone the whole time."

"I will," I said.

"You sound tired. Maybe you should get some rest before you have to go to work."

"I will."

"Then I'll let you go," Dad said, and I might have heard him yawn.

"Okay. I'll talk to you tomorrow." I hung up and set the phone on the coffee table. I kept expecting the phone to chime to alert me that I had a text message, but it remained quiet all afternoon. I went shopping and made dinner, then watched television. I wondered if I should call Ronnie, but I didn't. I'd said he needed a chance to think, and if he was doing that, then I needed to leave him alone. Hell, maybe he wanted me to leave him alone for good. I'd always known if things didn't work out that I could lose a friend. I guess I'd forgotten just how much that could hurt.

CHAPTER 6

My work schedule was messed up. Having to take a week off without any planning meant the work had stacked up and everyone wanted something from me. I usually got to the office early and left at four so I could meet the guys at the gym, but I found myself working late every night to try to catch up. My boss was sympathetic about why I'd had to take time off, but the work still needed to get done, and I did my best to catch up.

By Friday I was exhausted, but I was caught up and able to leave at my usual time. I got to my car and drove to Maryland to see my dad. He was in good spirits and seemed happy and alert. We talked for a few hours, part of it while he ate his dinner. Then we watched a baseball game, something he and I hadn't done since I was a kid. Granted, then Dad had taken me to the ballpark and fed me enough junk food that I'd nearly woofed in the car on the way home, something he reminded me of during one of the commercials.

After the last inning, Dad was tired, so I got ready to leave and checked in with the nurse's desk. They were concerned at how tired he seemed all the time, and I made a note to call Dad's doctor and check with him. They all said he'd be at the rehab center a few more weeks, but I was starting to have my doubts that Dad would ever be able to go home alone. Once Dad was asleep, I went back to his place, made sure it was cleaned for him, and went to bed.

My phone rang in the middle of the night, and I panicked until I saw the number. "Ronnie, do you know what time it is?"

"Yeah," he said. "Sorry to call, but I didn't know who else to talk to."

I groaned inwardly and forced my eyes to stay open. "It's okay." My eyelids were too heavy, but I forced my mind into gear. "What's wrong?"

"I can't stop it," he said.

"Stop what? Ronnie, you need to explain."

"What I remembered. I can't stop it. I thought I could forget it again like I had before, but it won't go away, and my head aches and I can't sleep. I haven't for days."

"Then you need to talk about it. You can't forget something that's bothering you. All you can do is let it go."

"I can't."

I could imagine Ronnie sitting on the edge of his bed with his head in his hands, talking on speaker, and I was at a loss about how to help him.

"When will you be back?" he asked.

"Tomorrow morning. I'm going to see Dad, and then I'll head home. I won't be there in time for the gym, but maybe for lunch."

He was quiet, and for a second I thought I'd lost the connection. "Okay," he whispered, softly enough that I could barely hear his response. "Why didn't you call me all week?"

"I was working late because of the time I was off helping with Dad." I didn't point out that his question went both ways. At this hour of the morning, I figured logic and reason had taken a backseat to whatever was going on in Ronnie's head. "Do you want someone there with you? I can call Jerry or Bobby."

"Those posers," he huffed, and I wondered what in the hell had happened. "I need this to stop."

"Have you taken your medication?" I hated asking that question, but the last time I'd seen him like this, he'd forgotten, and it took a while for his behavior to even out once again.

"Yeah. This isn't that." His voice changed, and then he was talking directly into the phone. I pictured him wandering through his house, going aimlessly from room to room. I had no idea if I was correct, but I couldn't shake the idea. "I think I need to tell you about it."

"Okay, you can tell me now if you want." I was wide awake now, and I sat up in the sofa bed. I hadn't been sleeping very well to begin with.

"No. This isn't a phone thing." He sighed.

"I'll come home in the morning and meet you at your house. Order some food, and when I meet you there, we can talk." I wondered what could possibly be so upsetting. Ronnie was one of those guys who talked. When something bothered him he told everyone about it—at the gym, in the sauna…. The thought of him keeping something bottled inside until he couldn't stand it any longer was frightening. "You need to go back to bed. Whatever you have to tell me, I'll listen, I promise, and I won't let you forget to tell me about it. So try to stop the wheels and just go to sleep." I remembered how I'd calmed him before.

"You promise?" he asked, sounding like a five-year-old.

"Of course. I always do what I say I'm going to do. Are you getting that gorgeous ass of yours back in bed?"

"Yes." His voice was lighter. "I always thought my ass was too big, you know. I have to buy special jeans because my legs and butt are wide. I can't wear those skinny things you buy." That Ronnie noticed my jeans was a pleasant surprise.

"Ronnie, you're the only man who's ever asked me if his pants make his butt look big. I told you then and I'll tell you now: your ass makes your pants look big and it doesn't fucking matter." I stopped short of telling him that his beefy ass and legs made for great gripping and the fuck of my life. The thought of it was making me hard, and I should've been ending the call to go to sleep. "So stop worrying about your ass and get into bed. I'll see you tomorrow, and we can talk all you like."

"You'll call me?"

"As soon as I leave in the morning." I waited for him to hang up, then placed the phone on the table, and lay back down. This whole situation was confusing as hell. I thought Ronnie was angry with me and hadn't been able to deal with what had happened between us, so I hadn't called, and he hadn't called because I hadn't called. It seemed like such a high school thing to do. But then again, Ronnie often acted like he was still in college, so maybe that was just him.

My phone beeped. I opened the message. There was a picture that I wouldn't have been surprised to be of his dick. It was a dark picture of him in bed, bare-chested. *Good night*, I sent in return and put my phone aside. Even if I lived to be a hundred, there would be things about him I was never going to understand. Maybe that was what attracted me to him in the first place.

I DID manage to sleep after our call, but I was up early, so I had breakfast with Dad and spent some time with him before heading out. He seemed in better spirits in the morning, which was great, and as I was leaving, the aide was taking him down for "his daily torture."

I pulled into Ronnie's drive a little after noon. Ronnie came out of the house as I pulled to a stop. He opened my door, and I followed him inside.

"Did you go to the gym this morning?" I asked.

"Yeah. The guys wanted to go to lunch, but I said I was busy." He closed the door. I walked through to the dining area, a little frightened at what I was going to see. I half expected a diet of cookies and candy, but he'd stopped at Wegmans and there were half a dozen salad packages in the center of the table.

"Do you want to talk first or eat?"

"I'm hungry," he said as he pulled out a chair. I got plates and silverware and grabbed waters out of the refrigerator while he opened the containers. I set down the dishes, and he began filling up his plate.

I took what I wanted and thanked God he remembered the macaroni salad, which I could eat by the gallon. "I get the feeling you're stalling. You know you've got me worried, because you talk about everything."

"Not this," he said softly. "You can never tell anyone about this."

I took a bite of salad and waited for him to come to the point, but he lowered his gaze and turned his attention to what he was eating.

"You know it isn't going to get easier to say," I said. "Does it have to do with you and me?"

Ronnie shook his head. "It's something that came back to me last week... you know...."

"You've never had a moment's trouble saying the words to anything."

"When we fucked. Okay? I remembered it when we were fucking. I don't know why, and it has nothing to do with you and me being together or anything."

I ate slowly and watched the stress build in Ronnie as the seconds ticked by. I set my fork down, feeling the nervous energy radiating from him. His eyes were huge, and if I didn't know better, I'd have wondered what drugs he was taking. "Are you sure you want to talk to me about this? Maybe your therapist or your mom would be a better idea." My heart told me this was something important. Ronnie didn't hold things in, and yet this—whatever it was—didn't want to be let out. It was so out of character for him that I wondered if I would be able to help him.

"I'm an action kind of guy," I said. "If you come to me with a problem, I'm going to try to help you any way I can. You know that."

Ronnie nodded. "This isn't that kind of problem, and you can't fix it or make it go away. No one can."

"Screw it," I said softly, pushing my plate away. I got up and began carrying all the food to the refrigerator and sliding it in. Then I took Ronnie's plate and mine and put them in the refrigerator as well. "Come on."

"Where are we going?"

"Just follow me." I led him into the living room. I hated the furniture he had. The stuff was all about design, but it was largely uncomfortable as hell. The formal living area was the only place in the house with decent, comfortable furniture. Well, at least as close as Ronnie's place got. I sat down and waited for him.

"Why not in there?"

"Just sit," I said. This room was darker, warmer, and the furniture deeper. It had a tone of serenity the rest of the house lacked. "You have my attention, and I'll listen to whatever you want to tell me." I had intended for him to sit on the sofa with me, but he took one of the chairs. "What did you remember?"

Ronnie nodded. "When it came back to me, I thought it must have been my imagination, but it hit me too hard, and the fear came back to me all at once."

I remembered that moment. I'd remained quiet at the time, but that had to be when he shook in my arms. "Take your time and tell me whatever it is."

"You can't tell anyone, not even my mother," Ronnie said. "She has enough on her plate, and she's just getting her life back together." He lifted his gaze from where he'd been studying the carpet at his feet and how the pile changed when he slid his foot over it. "I think she really likes Eric. She hasn't said anything, but it would be okay if she had someone in her life. I know she misses Dad as much as I do, but there's no reason she should be alone for the rest of her life."

"Focus on what you wanted to tell me," I said.

"My head swims when I get like this," Ronnie told me. "It used to drive Maggie crazy because when I got upset, my mind flew all over the place. I know her leaving was my fault. I drove her away." I was afraid he was going to break down, but I let him go where he wanted. If he needed comfort, I'd be there.

"Did you ever think maybe there isn't blame to assess? That neither of you is at fault? Sometimes relationships end, and that's okay. You weren't what the other needed. She has her issues, and you have yours. Let the past be the past and concentrate on the future. Do you remember how you felt when you and she were just going out?"

"Yeah, it was like heaven. She was so much fun but kind of broken. She needed me then, and I liked being there for her."

I wasn't going to go into it now, but Ronnie had taken control and Maggie had let him. She'd needed that. But as their relationship built, she got more confident and needed him less. "But relationships and people change, and sometimes they grow apart. You know that's okay, right? There doesn't have to be blame. It just happens."

"I guess." He didn't believe me.

"There's no guessing. It happens a lot, and that's what happened to the two of you. I know you miss her, but she wasn't making you happy any longer, and you weren't good for her either. Both of you are better off." I waited. "So let's get back to what you wanted to tell me."

"It's no big deal," he said and sat back in the chair.

I snapped my fingers because I knew he hated that. "You called me in the middle of the night because you were up and couldn't stop thinking about whatever this is. I think it's a big deal, and you're trying to hide. Don't."

Ronnie got up and walked out of the room. I heard his feet on the hardwood, getting softer and softer, but then he came back. "I know I have to, but what if—"

"There aren't any what-ifs until you tell me what has you pacing your own house like a spooked horse. You look as though you're going to run at any second and not stop until you collapse." I blinked a few times, feeling his torment and knowing I couldn't help unless he opened up. But I was equally afraid of what he was going to tell me. My imagination went in many different directions as a chill went up my spine.

He sat back down, and I waited once again. "I think I was about eight years old…." His phone rang, and I wanted to fucking scream. Ronnie snatched it off the table like it was a life preserver. "Hey, Jerry." He listened for a second. "I don't know." Ronnie put the phone aside. "They were asking if they could come over to play pool and hang out."

I extended my hand, and to my utter shock, Ronnie handed me his phone. "Jerry, it's Clay. Ronnie and I are going over some business this afternoon."

"Oh. I thought you were in Baltimore."

"I was. Ronnie and I had an appointment, so I came back. What we're discussing is confidential stuff, and it's going to take a while."

"Cool," he said. "We'll see you later."

"Definitely." I ended the call and turned to Ronnie. "Go on."

"But it would be fun if they came over."

"Maybe, but this is more important than them coming here to play pool or watch whatever movie or game is on." I got up and walked around to the back of his chair, placing my hands on his shoulders. "Just let go and tell me what happened. You were about eight."

"Yeah. We lived in New Jersey then. Dad had this really successful tire-distribution business, and he and Mom were going out for the night to a dinner they were throwing for customers. Mom didn't want to go, but Dad said they had to, so they got one of my cousins to babysit."

"On your mom or dad's side?" I asked.

"One of my dad's brother's kids. Blake. He came over, and Mom and Dad left and weren't going to be back until after midnight. I must have figured we'd watch TV or play Nintendo. But Blake wasn't interested and started making phone calls. Soon other kids were coming to the house and having a party."

"Did you call anyone?"

Ronnie grinned. "Why would I? They were nice enough and weren't hurting anything that I remember. Mostly talking and stuff. There were maybe six people. They were friends of Blake's, and he was nice. It was like I was a guest at a big kids' party. They were interesting and seemed cool. Anyway, when I started getting tired, Blake said everyone had to be quiet and took me upstairs. I didn't want to go to bed, but Blake said it was time and that everyone was going to be leaving anyway, so I got my pajamas on and went to bed."

Nothing sinister so far, but my skin crawled anyway.

"The house was quiet, and I remember hearing the front door open and close a few times and saw some of the people leaving. I figured the party was over and everyone had gone home. Blake was out front talking to a girl, and I was watching him as he kissed her and stuff." Ronnie began to fidget, and I knew he was getting to the difficult part of the story.

I took his hand. "You know I love you, and nothing that you say is going to change that."

"You do?" Ronnie asked.

"Of course I do." I didn't know how the words slipped out, but they were true, and I needed to say them as much as I thought he needed to hear them. "So just take your time."

Ronnie sat still, staring out of the room. "My door opened. I had been standing on my bed looking out the window. I turned around and saw one of the guys Blake had invited to the party. I told him Blake was out front with a girl. I remember making a face because I was eight and girls were yucky. He seemed to agree and walked over, leaning over the bed to look out. In my mind I hear him swearing." Ronnie held his head in his hands. "All of a sudden Pete—that was his name, Pete—hit me across the head. I fell down on the bed and then landed on the floor hard. I got up, and he hit me again. I don't know why, but he did, and this time everything went black and fuzzy."

"Maybe that's why you didn't remember until now," I suggested.

"I guess, but it's all so clear. I can see everything as though it was yesterday. Pete was really mad about something, and I think it was at Blake, but he took it out on me and hit me. My face hurt for days."

"You must have been bruised. Did you have a concussion or get sick when you woke up?" I asked, tempted to check him over even though what he was describing happened decades earlier.

"I didn't get sick, and my face was all red when I went into the bathroom."

"Now long were you out?"

Tears ran down Ronnie's cheeks. "I don't know, but when I woke up, my cheeks hurt and my pajamas were around my knees. I didn't know why, but my butt hurt too." He pulled his hand away and covered his face. I tried like hell not to gasp out loud. "I remember being dizzy and there was a bump on my head. I pulled up my pajamas and got some of the cream Mom kept in the bathroom and put it on my butt because that's what you did when your butt was sore."

"Did you cry?"

"Yeah. Blake came in and helped me back in bed. I don't think he knew what happened, but he soothed me and read me a story. I fell asleep, and in the morning I told Mom my head hurt, and she gave me a pill that made it feel better."

"And up till now, you didn't remember any of this?" I asked.

"No. I've thought about it, and I remembered nothing. I must have blocked it out or gotten my head scrambled when he hit me. It was blank until it snapped back, and I've been trying to figure out how I could have been abused and not remembered it."

"You were eight years old," I said, and my voice broke. The thought of Ronnie, or any kid, being powerless while someone hurt them.... "You did the best you could to protect yourself at the time. And Dolores never wondered if there was anything wrong?"

"I guess not," Ronnie said. "And now I'm trying to figure out how to deal with the fact that a friend of my cousin, a cousin I still see now and then at family gatherings, raped me."

I nodded. "Can I ask a few questions? Do you remember bleeding at all? Was the soreness on the inside, like after the first time we were together?"

"No, it didn't feel like that," Ronnie said.

"Okay. I'm not an expert, and short of someone taking you to the doctor when it happened to be sure, it's possible he might not have raped you. Chances are if he had, you would have bled, because you were a kid and you most likely would have been injured."

"So you're saying he... what?" Ronnie asked in a sharp tone. "I remember it now."

"You remember him hitting you, but do you remember the rest or is your mind filling it in?"

"I... I don't remember the rape."

"Then what I'm saying is that there's the possibility that he didn't do it. Yes, he hit you, and I'd like to use the asshole as a punching bag for that and anything else he might have done, but if he'd penetrated you, it would have hurt and you probably would have bled, which you say you didn't."

"Then why were my pants down?" Ronnie asked.

"Maybe he intended to, or came to his senses and realized what he was about to do and bolted. I only know what you've told me, and anyone who'd hit an eight-year-old kid like that has to be some kind of psycho."

"So you don't think I was—" Ronnie swallowed. "—raped."

"I don't know. I sure as hell hope not."

Ronnie jumped to his feet, startling me. "So if I had been, would that mean that you'd feel sorry for me and shit? Or that now I was tainted and dirty?" Ronnie began pacing again, and I let him talk, knowing all this was the result of what he was remembering and not really directed at me. "What if I did something? What if it was all my fault?"

"How could any of this be your fault? You were eight years old and someone hurt you. Someone your cousin shouldn't have allowed in the house in the first place." I wanted to strangle Ronnie's cousin. My hands clenched into fists that I pressed to my sides. "Is that what you were worried about? That you might have done something? Because I can say with certainty there is no way you did. No fucking way."

"I keep thinking that—"

"You know you didn't do anything."

"But what if I can't remember? What if this is only part of it and there's more?"

"Ronnie, you were eight. There's nothing you could have done to deserve that. Nothing at all. So forget all about trying to blame yourself or wondering what you did, because I know that answer... and so do you." I paused. "I can't imagine what it must have been like to have all this flood back after so long."

"At least you were there."

"You should have said something."

"I didn't know if it was real. To tell you the truth, I still don't. My head aches like hell right now."

"Close your eyes and put this all out of your mind for now. I'm going to get you something for your headache, and then we can talk some more."

"You're not going to leave?" Ronnie asked.

"I'll be right back." I left the room and walked through to Ronnie's bathroom. I'd seen a lot of bottles in there, and I found some ibuprofen and some Tylenol. I grabbed both of them and his bottle of water from the table. "Which do you want?"

He grabbed the Tylenol and took two. "What in the hell do I do now?"

"About what? I'm afraid that unless you want to hunt this Pete down and find out why he did what he did, there isn't much you can do. Have you thought about talking to your mom?"

Ronnie shivered. "God no. She doesn't know. If she did, she would have talked to me about it by now. Hell, she would have taken me to the doctor at the time. I still don't know if this is real or something my head mixed up in a weird way to fuck with me."

"Well, I believe you," I told him.

Ronnie nodded. "I'm going to lie down for a while. I'm wiped out."

"Are you hungry?" I asked. Ronnie shook his head and walked slowly to his bedroom. I was starving but didn't really want to sit around Ronnie's house while he was more than a little out of it. Above all, he needed rest. In the end I decided to stay around in case Ronnie needed me. I retrieved my plate and finished eating while standing at the kitchen island. I was putting my dishes in the sink when Ronnie came out and joined me. I heard his footsteps and turned around. He was naked, marvelously so, but looked miserable.

"What are you doing? The neighbors can see you."

"Then the lesbians over there can get the thrill of their lives," he quipped. "I don't want to be alone."

"Ronnie, this isn't a good idea at all." I tried like hell to turn away, but there was only so much restraint a guy could have. Ronnie's skin was golden, with a vine and thorn tattoo around one bicep. I had seen it more times than I could count, but right now in the sunlight, he glowed, and fuck if I didn't want to lick every line of his ink, continue down to his nipples, his ridged belly, and then to his cock, which stood straight and proud from between his legs.

"Why?"

My mouth went dry, and I tried to think of a reason, but the blood had drained south and away from my brain. "Because you just told me what happened to you, and I think sex is the last thing you need right now." I didn't add that sex with a guy probably wasn't a good idea. The last time it had brought forward this repressed memory. What if something else happened?

"How do you know what I need?" He stepped closer, his cock rocking back and forth like a metronome, and no way could I shift my gaze.

"Is this one of those 'trying to forget' times?" I asked, wondering how I felt about that. Yeah, it was flattering that I could get Ronnie hot enough and over the top with desire that his mind would stop its circling, but I also wondered if he was only interested in me for that ability.

"Jesus, it's one of those 'I'm really fucking horny' times." He grabbed my hand, and I put down the cloth I'd been using. I'd forgotten I still had it in my hand. I mean, I'd follow that meaty bobbing ass anywhere.

How he could go from broken up, shaking, and unsure, to horny and raring to go in about half an hour was beyond me. Not that I was going to complain, but I definitely didn't understand it.

Ronnie kicked the bedroom door closed and pushed me toward the bed. I sat down, and Ronnie tugged off my shirt. Up till now when we'd been together, I'd been the aggressor, which had bothered me a little. Ronnie had enjoyed himself, there was no doubt about that, but I'd always wondered if I was being too forceful. I realized I wasn't when Ronnie tugged my shirt up over my head. I had to kick my shoes off while Ronnie stripped me of my pants and underwear and tossed them to the floor. Then he stared at me as I sat naked on the side of the bed. "What do I do now?"

"Excuse me?" I said. "What do you want to do?"

He looked down at me.

"Just do what makes you happy. That's what sex is about."

He shrugged and pushed me back on the bed. Then he climbed on and straddled me. I knew what he wanted and guided Ronnie's cock to my mouth before sucking him deep.

"You're fucking good at that," Ronnie groaned, and I pressed my palms to his ass, steadying him as I bobbed my head, sliding his cock over my tongue.

"I know what you like," I whispered after inhaling deeply. Then I sucked him once again. I really hadn't expected Ronnie to be interested in sucking me, and that was fine. I was a master at oral sex, but it wasn't one of my favorite things. I generally needed more stimulation than oral sex provided. Ronnie, on the other hand, was in heaven. He had his hands behind his head, lengthening his body. He looked gorgeous stretched out above me, lips parted slightly. He looked down at me, and his eyes glazed over as I tightened my lips and sucked him completely into my mouth, holding him there.

Thanks to Maggie, I knew exactly what it took for Ronnie to come, so I was able to tease and lick, sucking on just the head and then his balls until Ronnie moaned like a ten-dollar whore. Then I pulled away and pushed Ronnie onto the bed. I crawled between his legs and sucked him once again, working a finger inside him. I had to be careful because Ronnie was already ramped up, and I wasn't ready for him to come yet.

"God, you always make me wait," Ronnie groaned as he thrust his hips forward.

"That's the fun part. I'm not one of the Sues who'll get you off as fast as she can. I like to watch the way your eyes widen and how your mouth hangs open because you're so into it. There's nothing better than that."

"Do you think I might get to fuck you someday?" Ronnie asked.

I opened him farther and searched in the bedside table for a condom. "If you're good," I answered wickedly. Nothing I'd ever experienced could compare to the moment I slid into Ronnie, those first few seconds when his breath hitched and his muscles gripped me like a vise. His heat surrounded me, pulling me deeper.

"You feel fucking huge," he told me.

I smiled. Just the words every man wanted to hear.

"God, how do you know—"

I changed the angle, and Ronnie gripped the bed as I rocked slowly in and out. I was determined to take my time, letting him work up a head-popping amount of erotic steam.

"Yes!" Ronnie screamed, and I thanked God the house was air-conditioned, because if the windows were open, the neighbors would be getting an earful.

"*Ronnie!*" I heard from the other side of the door.

"Jesus," I groaned.

"Don't you dare fucking stop!" Ronnie demanded and grabbed my ass, pressing to me hard. I put the distraction out of my head and drove into him. "Fucking hell yes!" Ronnie yelled, and whoever the hell was out there must have understood what was going on because the door stayed closed as I drove him home. When Ronnie came, he screamed at the top of his lungs and shot hard enough that come ended up in his hair, on his face, and trailed down his chest, the sight sending me plummeting over the edge.

"Fuck, you're incredible when you do that," I told him with a smile. I leaned forward and kissed him hard. "I meant what I said before, just so you know." I tried to catch my breath, my brain working again. "Did you hear someone call for you?"

Ronnie stilled completely and groaned. "Yes." He got out of the bed and raced to the bathroom. I smiled at his bobbing butt and covered up.

"What do you want me to do?" I knew this was a moment of truth. I was too damn old to be anyone's dirty little secret, and in a minute I was going to find out how Ronnie felt about… whatever was going on between us. I only wished I knew what it was. Were we simply fucking, or was he developing feelings for me? I felt like a teenager, and I thought I'd left that behind decades ago.

"Stay here," Ronnie said when he came out of the bathroom. He stepped into a pair of jeans and pulled them up, denying me the view, then tugged on a T-shirt before leaving the room. "Mom, what are you doing here?" I heard him ask through the cracked door.

"Are you back with the airhead you were seeing at the party? That girl didn't have the sense God gave a goose," she snapped.

Dolores certainly had the measure of Cherie.

"No. Mom, I think you need to sit down."

I got out of the bed and hastily began dressing. I didn't know what was going to happen, but I wasn't going to be caught bare-assed naked by Ronnie's mother in his bedroom.

"Who is it? Why isn't she out here? Are you ashamed of her?"

"Mom, sit down," Ronnie said.

I heard footsteps and was racing to tuck in my shirt and get my shoes back on when Dolores charged in the room like a bull elephant.

"Clay," she said, stopping. "I heard Ronnie in here with some girl. Wait, is she in the bathroom?" She turned to Ronnie, who was behind her. "What in the hell were you boys doing? Having a three-way?" She gaped at Ronnie while I put my hand over my mouth. "I always knew you were kinky, but I figured if you have three-ways, it would be with two girls." She turned back to me, and I schooled my expression and turned to Ronnie.

"There was no three-way, Mom," Ronnie said. "And you should call before you come over."

"Since when should I call before I visit you?" She gasped and stared daggers at me. "If there was no three-way, what was Clay watching?"

Ronnie took Dolores by the arm and guided her out of the room. That woman knew way too much about everything. I finished dressing and then followed them into the media room, where Ronnie sat on the curvy sofa next to his mother. It was the weirdest piece of furniture I had ever seen, and I had no idea how anyone could be comfortable with that awful curvy-back thing.

"You need to explain this to me," Dolores was saying.

"You should have called. But since you're here, what you heard was me and Clay," Ronnie said, looking straight at his mother.

"So you're into guys now?"

"I think what we were doing in the privacy of my bedroom is not something I want to discuss with you." Ronnie kept his voice very measured.

"I think you need to tell me what's going on. Are you gay now? Are you doing this to get back at me because I'm seeing Eric?" Dolores asked, and I instantly felt like an intruder on a family scene from a soap opera.

"You're seeing Eric? Is it serious?" Ronnie asked. I walked into the kitchen. Sometimes the way he switched topics on a dime was too much.

"I think so. We're exploring things, and we'll take it slow, but let's get back to the point at hand. You're saying you and Clay are having sex, or that you've had sex. I mean, there's nothing wrong with having sex with guys—I've done it my entire life. But this is a shock."

"Mom, it wouldn't have been if you'd called and I could have talked to you when I was ready to. And no, I don't think I'm gay. I like women. Always have."

"Okay, so you're bisexual. I can deal with that." I saw her look over at me and expected venom, but I only saw confusion. "But you should know not to mess around with your friends. This was just messing around, wasn't it?"

Ronnie hesitated and I held my breath. "I don't know. We've been together a few times, and things work really well. I kept wondering if I was gay, but Clay doesn't think so, and neither do I, because beautiful women still get things working."

"Then why can't you just be with them? I don't care if you're gay or want to be with guys, but what about your career? This is

Pennsyltucky, for God's sake. People can be as conservative as hell, and they aren't going to put their money with someone they don't approve of."

"My career is my work, not yours. And I don't really know what's going on, but I will tell you this: when I'm with him, the wheels stop turning and I can relax and actually think. I can't remember a time when everything didn't turn in my head, but it doesn't when I'm with Clay. So I don't know what's going to happen or how to define what's between us. I don't think he does either. But I will say that whatever it is, it's between Clay and me."

"Yes. But I'm your mother, and I'm only trying to understand what's changed all of a sudden. You never showed any interest in men before, and all of a sudden, from what I heard, you're going at Clay hammer and tongs."

"Mom...," Ronnie said, and I could hear the warning in his voice. The man was completely shameless, but I'd seen him like this before. If Dolores kept pushing, he was going to shut her up. Ronnie loved his mother and would do anything for her, but there were limits. "Just let it go. I am who I am, and you walked in on something that really isn't your business."

"You're my son. I worry about you. Sometimes you get impulsive and... what if you get hurt?"

"Clay isn't going to hurt me," Ronnie said with a conviction that warmed my heart. "He's the last person on earth who would ever hurt me. I thought it might have been you, but I was wrong." Ronnie got up and stormed into the bedroom, slamming the door.

Dolores settled back on the sofa and opened her purse, pulled out a file, and began looking at her nails. I brought in a bottle of water and handed it to her. "He'll be back in a few minutes." She was as cool and collected, as usual. "So what is going on?"

"I'm sorry, Dolores, but your guess is as good as mine. Things happened a few weeks ago, and they've kept happening. I have no idea how he feels, and I doubt he does either. I can't say anything more."

She stopped what she was doing. "You know, you're the one who stands to get hurt."

"I'm a big boy, Dolores. I've already been hurt and had my heart ripped to hell. Ronnie was the one who helped put me back together after Brian left. Whatever this is, we'll figure it out on our own."

"Mom, I want you to drop it," Ronnie said as he strode out of the bedroom.

"I'm just concerned." She'd pushed too far—I saw it in the set of Ronnie's jaw.

Ronnie walked right over to her and put his face inches from hers. "Please leave it alone. If I'm gay or bi, that's my business. And if I want Clay to fuck me until I can't see straight eight times a day, that's my business and his. I love you, and I already know you adore Clay, so just let it go. It's a shock, but it is what it is."

She stared at Ronnie and then at me, and I could only imagine her trying to process what Ronnie had said. She was quite a lady and demonstrated it once again. "Sometimes you share way too fucking much." Ronnie came by his mouth honestly.

"You wouldn't let it go," Ronnie told her.

"All right." She put away her file and closed the purse.

"You're really okay with this?" I asked her.

"What choice do I have? I always knew I raised an open-minded son. I guess I didn't know how open-minded." She patted my cheek. "Be good to one another. That's all I ask." She turned to Ronnie. "And you, remember that in any relationship, you aren't the most important thing. Most of the time it's about we rather than me." Ronnie didn't seem interested, and his mother smacked him on the arm. "I'm serious."

"I know that."

Dolores turned to me, and I got the message loud and clear, leaving the room as fast as I could. They needed some privacy, and I needed a chance to digest what I'd heard. I wasn't sure if our mutual confusion about what was going on between us was good or not. It would be nice if one of us understood what the hell was happening. I certainly didn't. Yet Ronnie had told Dolores that he knew I'd never hurt him. So did that mean he wanted me in his life as more than a friend or a fuck buddy? My head hurt as I pondered what all this meant. Of course I got nowhere and stood in the kitchen just as confused and turned around as I'd been when I'd first arrived a few hours ago.

"You listen to me, Ronald Sebastian Marvelli." Dolores's voice could carry through concrete. "You will listen to me. Maggie couldn't take any more because everything got to be about you. Yes, you work hard and make a lot of money, and sometimes that makes you think you're some hotshot big shot. But you're not too old to take over my knee, and dammit, I will if you act like an ass again. I don't care if you have a relationship with a man or a woman. Though I am shocked at the man part."

"You're shocked? I'm stunned. I'd never thought of being with a guy, but Clay knows what I need when I don't."

They got really quiet, and I was ashamed to say I leaned closer, listening as intently as I could.

"Then you hang on to him for all you're worth. You only get one chance in life to find someone who knows you better than you know yourself. I had that with your father, and if you have a chance at that, then man, woman, horse, fucking orangutan, you hang on to it for dear life, because once it's gone, it never comes back."

I left the kitchen and wandered into the dining room with a bottle of water, quietly sitting at the table, looking out the windows. Dolores came in. She didn't say a word, but she took my hand, squeezed it, and then left, closing the door quietly behind her.

I sat in the chair, seriously thinking it was time I went home. Nothing had gone the way I'd expected—not what Ronnie had told me, not the mind-blowing sex, followed by his mother practically walking in on us, and not Ronnie's coming out of sorts.... I was starting to wonder if my life was turning into a circus and I had been cast as the lion tamer—or was it the clown? I had yet to find out.

CHAPTER 7

FOR THE next few weeks, things stayed very much the same. I saw Ronnie a few times during the week, and sometimes after dinner with the guys, we'd go back to his place—once he came to mine—and we'd do our best to scream the walls down. We talked some, but I wasn't going to delve deeply into what this thing with Ronnie meant. I knew I should. But I kept wondering if he thought this was still just sex. If it was, I could deal with it, but I really didn't want to know. Not yet. As long as I didn't ask him outright about his feelings, there was still hope that he truly cared about me. If ignorance was bliss, then what I was doing was stupidity personified.

I visited my dad every Friday night after work and came home on Saturday. Ronnie would call as I was driving home, like clockwork, and we'd end up at his place. I began packing extra clothes in my gym bag so on Sunday morning we'd both meet the guys as though nothing was happening. I was in total denial, but I took heart in the fact that Ronnie hadn't hidden our connection from his mother, so I figured when the time was right, we'd talk to the rest of the guys. Not that I was particularly interested in those Chatty Cathys knowing my business anyway.

"Are you coming to lunch?" Jerry asked as we all headed to the locker room after our Sunday workout. "My sister Chrissy is visiting."

Bobby bumped my shoulder. "She's superhot."

Jerry glared at him and puffed out his chest. "None of you is to touch my sister." He stopped walking and turned to Bobby. "Don't even look at her funny. You hear me? She's sitting next to Clay and Phillip at lunch."

"Who is?" Ronnie asked, clapping Jerry's shoulder.

"Apparently his sister is joining us for lunch, and Jerry is fearful of her virtue, so he wanted Phillip and me to cock block for all the horniness he perceives you all exude." I couldn't help teasing him.

"Your sister is fine, and she could do worse than Ronnie or me," Bobby said. "You know it. So lighten up."

"Is she going to meet us?"

"Yeah, I just need to tell her where. She said she and a friend were going to be there."

"They'll treat your sister right," I told Jerry. "You know that. Everyone's giving you a hard time because you're being such a—"

"Douche," Bobby supplied, and while I wouldn't have used that word, it was an accurate description.

"I was going to say big brother, but douche works." Bobby and I shared a laugh. "Just relax. Everything is going to be fine, and your sister will go home with her virtue intact."

"Not if I get my hands on her," Ronnie said, doing a little hip thrust. Jerry groaned, and then Bobby hooted.

"See? You'd keep your sister away from Ronnie." Bobby grinned, and Jerry turned away with a moan only I heard. We reached the locker room, and I changed into my bathing suit and headed for the sauna. Ronnie was already in there talking to the guys, relating one of his stories about the time he picked up girls with a friend in Atlantic City and had the night of his life.

"Was that the best time you ever had?" I asked him, catching his gaze and seeing him swallow. The story faltered for just a few seconds, and then Ronne picked up his train of thought, ignoring my question. None of the guys picked up on it, and I knew it was a little childish, but hearing him talk about those times made me wonder if he didn't want them back, and if I wasn't just some temporary diversion until he reverted to women once again. After all, he'd been with them for decades and loved them. Or at least he loved sex with them, judging by his stories.

I pulled my attention from the story and sat back, letting the heat settle in. When the guys around me laughed and Ronnie's story ended, I expected another, but a number of the men got up to leave, and the room pretty much emptied out.

"Are you coming back to the house after lunch?" Ronnie asked.

I sighed. "I don't know. I need a chance to rest awhile before I go back to work."

"You can rest at my place, and we can watch a movie or something."

"All right." I was sweating up a storm as I stood to leave. Ronnie stayed behind, and I showered quickly before taking a dip in the whirlpool. When I was done, I met Ronnie as he was leaving the sauna. I tried not to gape as he dropped his shorts and stepped into the last shower. I knew I shouldn't, but I took the shower directly across from his. Ronnie grinned at me, stroking himself hard before snapping the curtain closed.

"Tease," I whispered. I heard him chuckle. Then he started the water, and I climbed into my shower and removed my suit. Just those few seconds with him had me excited. I turned on the water a little colder than normal to cool off and then continued with my shower. Of course once I was done and pushed my curtain back, I found Ronnie standing in his stall, shamelessly showing off everything Mother Nature had given him. I reached for my towel. "Do you want everyone to know what's going on?" I asked him. "Because if you do, just keep that up, and I'll give the entire gym something to watch." I stared at his dick and then into his eyes before raking my gaze down his body. "That ass of yours is looking mighty fine."

He swallowed and turned off the water, reaching for his towel as the other guys came in. I wrapped mine around my waist and left the room, trying like hell not to let my excitement show under my towel. Of course I'd forgotten that Ronnie had a locker just a few down from me, so he walked in and dropped his towel, getting out his clothes without looking at me or anyone else. I knew the little shit was doing it on purpose, and I thought of ways to make him pay... later.

I dressed as fast as I could, avoiding the towel fight Jerry, Bobby, and Phillip were having. They ran around in their pants, snapping and chasing each other. "Guys," I called, but they ignored me. I grabbed my towel, rolled it up, and snapped Jerry on his jeaned ass. He yelped and grabbed his butt, dropping his towel. "You have nothing on me, and that was through your jeans."

"Jesus," Jerry whined as he rubbed his ass.

"Then get dressed. We're supposed to meet your sister for lunch, remember? You're obviously worried about her virtue but not about being on time." I put my towel in my bag and got out my shoes and socks.

"You're deadly with that," Ronnie said, indicating the towel.

"Yes. And don't forget that the next time you decide to play show-and-tell in the shower...." The implication was that he better not be doing it with anyone but me. "That ass of yours might look good with little purple highlights," I told him in a whisper. Not that I was really into that sort of thing, but I loved the look on Ronnie's face: eyes wide and mouth open. Then he twisted his lips into a smile.

"You're funny, and that's way too kinky for you."

"Is it?" I retorted before lowering my gaze and pulling on my socks. "You have no idea what kind of kinky things I'm into." I liked teasing him a little. "Come on," I added, pulling on my shoes. "Let's get ready to go. I'm starving." I closed my bag and stood, grabbing it and then waiting for Ronnie to get his stuff. We walked together to join the others. "Where are we going?" I asked Jerry.

"Bonefish," he answered. "It's where Chrissy asked to go. Is that all right?"

"Are they open for lunch?" I asked, and he nodded. The guys went to their cars, and I walked with Ronnie toward where we'd parked.

"You aren't interested in lunch, are you?" Ronnie asked.

"Not really. I need some quiet, and these guys are anything but quiet. However, I'm not going to disappoint Jerry, so I'm going to go and have a good time." I unlocked my car and popped the trunk, then placed my bag inside.

I followed Ronnie to Bonefish. The guys were already inside, and I was introduced to Chrissy. She was in her early twenties and indeed attractive, with incredible wheat-yellow hair that cascaded to her shoulders, nice eyes, and great cheekbones. Her friend Monica, however, was model gorgeous, with raven hair, massive brown eyes, and a flawless complexion. Introductions were made, and we all sat, with Monica sliding in next to Ronnie and Chrissy next to me.

The server took drink orders once we were all set. "So what's it like to have Jerry as a brother?" I asked.

"About what you'd expect. He's pretty decent in a Neanderthal sort of way." I liked her right away. "Whenever I bring a date home, he feels it's his duty to make sure they behave." She smiled wickedly. "So of course I bring home the most motley crew of guys I can find. He scares them off, thinking he's some really big man, while I'm really dating someone else."

I laughed out loud.

"Don't say anything. He thinks I have the worst taste in men. It isn't true, but the dumb lug has to have something to make him feel useful."

"My lips are sealed," I told her.

"Do you have a boyfriend right now? Jerry told me you're gay."

"I don't know what I have right now, to tell you the truth. The guy I'm sort of seeing is probably more like a fuck buddy than anything else. But I have no idea." I did my best not to look at Ronnie. Chrissy was smart, and I was sure she'd pick up on it.

Monica giggled, and I looked down the table. She was hanging on Ronnie's arm, whispering in his ear and then simpered softly. I wanted to reach across the table and snatch her bald. I turned back to Chrissy and cringed inwardly. I was sure she'd seen. "Sometimes I think my life sucks," I said.

The waitress brought drinks and then took our orders. I was relieved for the interruption and thankful for the chance to school my expression. Not that it did much good. Monica placed her order and managed to chuckle and flip her hair at least twice doing it. Every time I heard that sound, my teeth grated. She had a hand on Ronnie's arm and leaned close to him, and the fucker leaned back.

"Do my brother and his friends know?" Chrissy whispered from next to me.

I turned toward her. "Of course not. They're all completely clueless." She smiled and rolled her eyes.

"Clueless about what?" Jerry asked.

"Life in general," Chrissy told him. "I swear if you ever got a clue, you could find the most amazing girl and get married, but instead you're as dumb as a stump when it comes to women, and you're alone ogling girls who might like you if you actually used your brain."

"Jesus," Jerry whined.

"You did ask. So don't ask stupid questions you don't want to know the answers to." She winked at me, and I nodded. I really liked this girl.

"Honey, if I weren't gay, I think you'd be the girl of my dreams," I told her, and she laughed.

"That's my sister," Jerry said puffing up.

"He's gay, get a clue," Chrissy told him, and Jerry backed off. "You're such a caveman." The last comment was delivered without humor, and Jerry mumbled something under his breath. "He thinks he needs to watch out for me when I'm perfectly capable of taking care of myself." I wasn't getting in the middle of this, and just then another giggle raked up my spine like nails on a chalkboard. I did my best to ignore it and just eat my salad when it arrived.

The guys talked about this and that, with Jerry keeping dutiful, if unwanted, watch over his sister. It was sweet in a way, and he clearly cared about her a great deal; otherwise he wouldn't have bothered.

Ronnie told stories. "Last week I was downtown, and the place was rocking. I pulled up in front of Café Fresco, and one of their valets moved their loading-zone sign and waved me into the slot right in front. They love having the Lambo parked out front."

"Does that happen a lot?" Monica asked.

"Sure it does, baby. I get that kind of treatment all the time," Ronnie said, as though he were a Hollywood icon. I wanted to smack him, and in that instant, like the proverbial lightbulb coming on, I realized what a stupid fool I'd been. Ronnie was who he was. I wasn't going to change him, and he wasn't going to change for me. It didn't matter what kind of sex we had or who he told, Ronnie liked women, and expecting him to change the behavior of decades just because he'd had sex with me a few times was completely ridiculous. I'd been stupid enough to fall in love with him, a largely straight guy, and now I was jealous as hell when he paid attention to a beautiful woman.

"You're grinding your teeth," Chrissy said. "Are you okay?"

"Just dumb as shit." Suddenly, I couldn't get enough air, and I had to get the hell out of there. I quickly pushed back my chair, and one of the legs must have caught on something because it began to topple. I could feel it, I knew what was happening, but damn if I could stop it. The chair hit the floor, and I couldn't manage to catch myself before I completely went with it.

I cringed in embarrassment and got back up as everyone in the restaurant turned to look at me. The guys were laughing because, well, they were the guys and had the maturity of eight-year-olds. Chrissy helped me to my feet, and I righted the chair. What hurt most was Ronnie laughing along with the rest, like in one of those movie sequences where everything becomes distorted. I snatched up my napkin, placed it on the chair, and walked as quickly as I could without running toward the parking lot.

As soon as I was outside, I sucked in air. I wanted to go home and hide for a while, but my friends were inside and…. Dammit. I could feel the tears I didn't want under any circumstances threatening. Fuck it all to hell, I was a man, not a child, and I would be damned if anyone was going to see me break down like a girl.

"Are you all right?" a man asked as he burst through the door.

"Yes." It wasn't Ronnie like I'd hoped. I assumed it was the manager. "Just a little clumsy, I guess. I didn't hurt anything but my pride."

"Are you sure?" he asked.

I nodded. "I didn't hurt myself," I told him softly. "Thank you. I just wanted to step out for some fresh air, and I didn't mean to cause anyone any trouble." I felt like a fool in so many ways. "Please don't let me keep you." He nodded and went back inside. I stood out front for a few minutes and then went back inside myself.

I returned to the table, and everyone had the decency to continue their conversation. I sat back down and finished my salad just in time for my main dish to arrive. I'd ordered tilapia and ate part of it, but my appetite had gone in my spill. The others talked, and Chrissy sort of kept an eye on me, pulling me into the conversation.

It was Phillip who approached me after we were done. "Are you really okay?"

"I'm fine. The chair tipped, that's all."

I glanced over at Ronnie, who was still talking with Monica outside the restaurant. Chrissy joined them, and then she said good-bye to everyone, hugged Jerry, and guided her friend toward their car.

"Are we going to do something?" Jerry asked.

"Not me," Ronnie said. He finally looked at me. "You guys go have fun, though." Ronnie said his good-byes and walked to his car. I said my good-byes and got in my car, then pulled out of the lot. I knew Ronnie was expecting me to go back to his place, but I was in no mood, alternating between self-doubt, anger, and heartbreak. So instead of turning toward Ronnie's, I went right home.

I parked out front and was walking to my door when I heard the unmistakable sound of Ronnie's car. He pulled to a stop right behind me and got out. I unlocked my door and went inside, leaving it open for him.

"What's going on?" Ronnie demanded as soon as he was inside. "I thought we were going back to my place for the afternoon."

"Why would I do that?" I dropped my bag on the floor. "Look, Ronnie, this isn't going to work. Whatever you're playing at… it's just that: playing for you." I sighed. "This whole thing is my fault, and I'm the one who let things get way out of hand."

"You're breaking up with me?" Ronnie asked.

"There's nothing to break up. You and I hooked up a few times, but that's all it was. You know that. I let this get out of control, and now you...." All I wanted was to save our friendship somehow. It had meant so much to me, and it still did, but I couldn't see a way of keeping it. "I pushed you into something you weren't ready for and didn't really want." I turned away and snatched up my bag, hoping he'd leave and I could nurse my pain in peace.

"What the fuck are you talking about? You think I'm a child? No one makes me do what I don't want to do. Not in a very long time, anyway."

"Fine, Ronnie, whatever you say. But that doesn't mean you want or need you and me to be together. This... whatever was between us—neither of us can seem to figure out what it is... or was.... God, how in the fuck should I know? It was a recipe for disaster. You don't want me other than as some sexual diversion. I can see that now. When you get tired of being with me, you'll go back to acting the way you always have. And why should you do anything different? You like women. It's what makes you happy."

"I do like women, and I have for a long time, but I also found out I like you... and I notice guys too. I've just never done anything about it with anyone but you. Does that make me wrong or something?"

My gym bag hit the floor again. "Of course not. But anything between us is doomed, and I want to salvage some of our friendship before that's completely gone. I told you I won't say anything to anyone, and you can continue impressing women and luring them into your bed. It's what you've always done, and I can't expect you to change no matter how much I might want you to." The only thing that kept me from breaking down was the adrenaline that coursed through me, but I could feel the rush of power that gave me the courage to say what I had to say ebbing away.

"So now I don't know my own mind or my own feelings, is that it?" Ronnie asked, his expression pinching.

"You sure acted that way at lunch. If that airhead Monica simpered one more time, I was going to beat the crap out of her. And you soaked it up like a sponge. Not that anyone could blame you. It's how you've been your whole life."

"What do you want from me?" Ronnie asked with a touch of exasperation mixed with confusion.

"I don't want anything from you. That's what I'm saying." At least that was what I thought I was saying. I had made a complete mess of things. "You need to live your life in a way that will make you happy… and I don't think that's with me." I deserved to be happy too, and if I didn't walk away from this now, I was going to join the ranks of every gay guy who'd gotten his heart broken by a man he shouldn't have fallen in love with in the first place.

"I was just talking to her."

I took a deep breath to calm my racing pulse. "Yes, but can you tell me that you didn't want to take her back to your place and drill her through the mattress? By the way she was hanging on you, that's what she wanted too."

That gave Ronnie pause. "Maybe I did. She was hot. But I didn't invite her back. Instead I got in my car and made sure no one would be around so I could spend the afternoon with you."

My shoulders slumped. "That's really nice, and I know you thought that was what you should do. But I don't want to be a secret. I need to live my life in the open. Brian might have turned out to be a shit, but we were together and didn't hide it. That's what I want: someone who will love me for me and do it in the open."

"I told my mother," Ronnie said weakly.

"I know you did, but only because she nearly walked in on us. You're a good man, and that's why I like you. You don't lie or cheat. Being deceptive isn't in your nature. But you feel you have to keep me a secret. And I understand it. I really do. But I can't live that way. I don't want to wonder every time a women flirts with you if that's going to be the time you decide being with another man is a bad idea."

"We've only been… fucking for a few weeks. You said yourself that you don't know what's going on. I don't either."

"That's true. But when you go out with a woman, for a night or just a few weeks, do you keep it a secret, or do you sit next to her at lunch and make her feel special? Do you only spend time alone with her when you're conveniently able to make sure the guys aren't going to be over for the afternoon? No. You have her meet your friends, maybe take her out for dinner…. I don't know what the hell you do, but you don't keep her locked in a closet out of sight." I swallowed hard, hoping I'd explained things clearly.

"So what do you want me to do?" Ronnie snapped.

"Nothing. You don't have to do anything at all. I'm letting you off the hook. Not that there ever was one. I don't think you're ready for a relationship with another guy. Great sex is one thing, but making him part of your life—your partner—is quite another." I paused and noticed that Ronnie didn't correct me. "I want more than someone to have sex with. I'm ready for a relationship with someone I could love for the rest of my life."

Ronnie turned away, and I figured he was about to leave. "You thought you could love me? Are you in love with me?"

"For the last few weeks I haven't been able to figure anything out. You're my best friend, and you helped me pull myself back together after Brian left. Of course I love you. I have for a long time. Maybe I got carried away and hoped that you could love me too."

"I do…," Ronnie whispered.

"No. I mean in the way I need to be loved—openly, honestly, and like I'm the most important person in the world. But your mom is right: the most important person in your world is you. And that's okay, I see that now. And I can't expect you to be something you aren't." I sat down on the sofa. "Like I said, this is my fault. I set us up for failure because I wanted you. I still want you." I had to turn away so Ronnie didn't see me fall apart. "But you don't know what you want, and how could you? It's not fair of me to expect you to change for me or anyone else." I took a deep breath. "I've spent my

131

life fighting to be who I am. I was too different to be popular in school and I didn't care."

"I was always popular," Ronnie said, his small attention span taking over once again.

"Of course you were. You have a personality that's huge, and people want to be around you. You're used to being the center of attention. That's who you are. The thing is, I fought to be myself, and I can't expect you to be any different from who you are." I could barely talk. "I think I've said all I can." My throat hurt, and I wanted to be alone.

"You know, you'll always be my friend," Ronnie said, stepping closer. "I was there for you when Brian left, and you were there for me when my dad died and then when Maggie left. I know I can be a handful."

I sniffled and jumped to my feet, hugging Ronnie tight. "I like who you are, and I don't want you to be any different for me. But that's what I've been doing." I kissed him on the cheek. "You didn't do anything wrong. I want you to know that. I was the one who had expectations and hopes that I shouldn't have had." I released him and stepped back. "I've loved you for a long time. I don't know when I started, but I do. And I love you enough to walk away before things get too intense for both of us."

"And you just decided all this," Ronnie snapped in a tone I'd never heard before. "You figured all this out by your fucking self." I'd seen Ronnie angry and hurt, but never at me. "You know what's best for me, do you? Well, fuck off." He glared daggers at me. "I happen to have a head of my own. In fact, I have two, and believe it or not, I know how to think with the big one. You may not think so, but I do." He stepped closer, and I took one step back to stay out of any potential line of fire. "You didn't talk me into doing anything I didn't want. I'm not gullible or stupid like you seem to think I am. And yes, I was having a good time at the restaurant with Monica, but she's a flirt, so I flirted back. But what do I care? I wasn't going to go home with her, and in fact I was looking forward to watching television and just being lazy with you. Does that sound like someone who's only interested in sex?"

His voice kept getting louder, and I didn't know what was going to happen next. "You're going to tell me that you were willing to tell the guys and everyone about us? Would you have taken me out on a date?"

"Of course I would. What did you think I am, a pig?" He inhaled and stared at me, hard. "You do. You think I'm a complete pig when it comes to women, and you expected me to act that way with you." He shook his head. "Well, screw you, Mr. Sanctimonious. Have I ever treated you badly? Or given you any cause to think I was ashamed of you or the fact that we've been together?" He calmed down a bit, and I hoped the storm was over. "You touched something inside me that no one else ever could, and I don't mean physically."

"I know that. Being with you was amazing. Why do you think this is so damn hard?" Fuck it all. I was on the verge of tears again and turned away. "I fucking fell in love with you, okay? You've always been there for me. I've loved you for years, and when I said what I said in the hotel, it was in a moment of weakness. I never expected you to agree, and I didn't expect things to be so mind-blowing. But you love women, and that isn't going to change."

"So what? Don't I get to fucking choose what I want and who I want in my life?"

"Sometimes not. Sometimes things don't work out, and I saw that this afternoon. Don't you see? If I had been the one who was foremost in your mind, you wouldn't have paid any attention to her. You'd have only had eyes for me. But you'll never do that. And I need to deal with that and try to move on."

Ronnie seemed to deflate.

"You need to realistically ask yourself if you want people to think you're gay, because if you're with a man, that's what they're going to think. Suddenly you turned gay, and that could affect everything in your life, including your work."

"I do love you."

I so needed to hear that right now. "Thank you," I whispered as Ronnie opened the door and left the house. As soon as he closed the door behind him, I sat down on the sofa, staring at the wall. I kept waiting for the disappointment and loneliness to hit me. It didn't right away.

I heard a drip in the kitchen and went in, turning off the sink all the way. Then I got my gym bag and carried it to the basement before starting a load of laundry. It wasn't until I sat on the sofa once again, listening to the hum of the air conditioner as it kicked in, that I realized what I'd done. I was alone again. After Brian left, I went through weeks of depression. I'd always been fine when I was on my own, but after eight years of company and having someone to watch television with and talk to, not having that had thrown me for a loop. It took a while to become comfortable with my own company. I felt exactly that same way right now.

Ronnie was still my friend, I hoped, and I'd still see him and the guys. I shook my head as reality hit. That wasn't possible. Things with Ronnie would never be the same, and by extension, even though the guys didn't know, things would be different with them as well. They had to be. So, instantly, that same loneliness that I felt after Brian left washed over me like a wave. Then I'd had my friends for support, but now I'd managed to fuck that up too.

I turned on the television for company but didn't really watch it. Eventually I grabbed one of the pillows off the sofa and held it to my chest. After a while of staring and doing nothing, I called my dad to make sure he was okay. I couldn't explain to him what was going on. But hearing him sounding stronger and having him tell me that he had an appointment with the doctor tomorrow and was hopeful he'd be going home soon was good news that had me smiling.

"When you're discharged, I'll come down and get you, and you can stay here for a week or so if you like." I wanted company, and it would be good for Dad to be around people.

"Helen from next door has already said she'd come sit with me in the afternoons. She and I play cards, and they're arranging for a nurse to come in a few days a week, along with a home support person who'll clean and things. That's only for a few weeks, but I need to be here."

"It's all right, Dad. Of course you do." I tried to keep the disappointment out of my voice.

"You don't need me there interfering with your life."

"Dad."

"I know you don't see it that way, and I love you for that, but I would be, and I have my friends here. Once I'm out of here, I'll be just fine."

"I know you will." I would have liked the company. "Let me know when you hear something, and I'll plan to be down to visit this weekend." We talked for a few more minutes. I felt even lonelier once I'd hung up. My dad, who'd had a stroke, was moving forward and getting on with his life better than I was.

Eventually something on television caught my attention, and I sat still for much of the afternoon, trying to get engrossed in whatever was on. For dinner I heated up a can of soup and watched more television in the evening. I kept hoping my telephone would ring or chime with a message from Ronnie telling me that I'd been wrong about everything. I probably would have believed it, but the phone remained quiet all evening, and finally I went up to bed.

CHAPTER 8

I WAS right, and for once in my life, I hated it. Things were so different. There were no texts to arrange times to meet at the gym and no invitations to dinner. When we saw each other, I think Ronnie and I both tried to pretend that everything was fine, but we could have cut the tension with a knife. I started avoiding him. The week was pretty much a hell of loneliness and avoidance. My dad did return home, and he was doing well. When I arrived for my usual Friday night visit, he had company, and apparently he'd had all he could want all day. The ladies brought him food and had even developed a schedule so they didn't overlap.

"How do you rate, Dad?" I asked when I saw the full refrigerator: juice, vegetables, fruit, salads, chicken—everything he could eat and plenty of it.

"I'm a single man in a condo complex full of retirement-age widows. I've never been this popular in my entire life." He grinned as I heated up a container of homemade chicken soup that turned out to be a bowl of heaven. "How are you, Clay? You seem down."

"I'm okay, Dad."

"Are you dating?"

"Not right now," I answered honestly.

"It's been long enough. You need to find someone and be happy."

My dad settled on the sofa, and I moved the tray closer so he could see the television and not spill. Apparently my father, who had always insisted we eat at the table growing up, liked to eat in front of the television now. Once he was settled, I sat down to eat.

"You know, I think Kathy from upstairs has a son who's gay," he said, "and she was telling me that he isn't seeing anyone right now.

He's quite a bit younger than you, I would imagine, but I suppose that doesn't matter so much. Age is only a number."

"Dad, I don't need you trying to fix me up, and yeah… it kind of does." I was not going to have a conversation about me trying to keep up with a twenty-five-year-old or something. "Just eat and relax. It's not your job to find me a husband."

"I want you to be happy before I slip off this mortal coil."

"Hopefully that's going to be quite a while from now." I hated it when Dad talked like that, and he'd been doing it more often lately. "You have a good life, and you aren't in any hurry, are you?"

"No, I'm not in a hurry." He exaggerated rolling his eyes. "But there is one thing I would like very much, and that's a grandchild. I know we've never talked about it much, and I don't want to say it's a regret, just an unfulfilled dream."

"Brian and I talked about it a few times."

"I know. But he wasn't right for you. Brian was too wrapped up in himself and what he wanted." Dad dropped his bombshell and then ate as though it was nothing.

"I thought you liked Brian."

"The man was a jackass," Dad said between bites. "He was selfish, and he didn't treat you right. I know you loved him, but he was a piece of work. You always stood up for him, and it pissed me off. Remember how he'd always send back his silverware in a restaurant? He barely looked at it but said he wanted clean. I hated going out with him. Normal people don't do that all the time. And let's not forget the way he'd scream if a cat came near him. Yeah, he was allergic, but you'd think they were coated in arsenic." Dad smiled evilly. "I was thinking of getting a cat so he'd stay away."

"Dad, he wasn't that bad."

He set down his spoon with a clang and stared at me. "Yes… he… was. Brian was a self-centered bastard, and the only person who couldn't see it was you. You loved him. I don't know why. But you did, and that was enough for me to put up with him. But now it's time for you to find someone nice, who cares about you. Someone like that

137

guy who brought you to the hospital and stayed with you all those hours. That's a caring person."

I did my best to cover my sigh and ate my soup. "Ronnie is a good friend."

"Don't try to fool me, young man," Dad scolded. "I'm not blind. You like him, and more than just as a friend. I liked him. You should have heard him on the phone at the hospital. He has a mouth on him that would make a sailor blush. "

"That he does."

"But he makes you smile," Dad said, and I realized I was smiling just thinking about Ronnie. "That's precious. You thought about him just now and smiled."

"I know. But it's complicated. Dad, he's straight… or mostly straight."

"But he cares about you."

"Yes, he does, and I love him. There's the problem. He also likes women."

"So he's bisexual. Big deal. I think if I were younger, I might give the other side a whirl to see what the fuss is all about."

I nearly did a spit take. "Dad, please. You like boobs way too much to ever give them up. And don't argue with me. When you meet a woman, you always check out the rack. Guys don't have boobs, Dad."

"Some do," he retorted and laughed. "And I was only making a point. Sexual roles aren't as defined as they were when I was young. You were either straight or a nancy boy, nothing in between. We know a lot more now, and I think your friend with the loud mouth might be one of those people who falls in the middle."

"Me too, but it doesn't matter. Women are central to his life, and I can't expect him to give them up on a dime. A lifetime of programming, habits, and behavior can't be changed just like that. Besides, we tried things and—"

"He sucked in the bedroom?" I couldn't believe I was having this conversation with my father. "Because let me tell you, there's nothing worse than going to bed with a dead fish. When we first married, your mother made me make sure every door in the house and the bedroom was locked and bolted before I could touch her. But soon that woman turned into a tiger, and I thank the Lord for it every day of my life. God, I miss her," he added in a whisper.

"I'm never having sex again," I muttered. "And since you asked, no, he was amazing in the bedroom. Head-exploding good."

"Please. You're proof that your mother and I had sex at least once. Clare and I wanted more children, but she miscarried three times, and we stopped after that. It was too hard on her physically and emotionally." Dad finished his soup and sat back on the sofa with a small sigh. "Let me ask you this, and it may sound weird."

"More weird than you talking about your sex life? I'm not sure that's possible."

"Smartass," Dad groaned. "You care about this guy, and you seem to have it going on in the bedroom." Dad paused. "Did I just say that? I need to watch less television."

"Daaad."

"Fine, just tell me what happened," Dad said, and I did. I told him everything, from how things began to how they ended. "You know, son, it sounds to me as though you chickened out."

"No, I didn't. It wasn't going to work."

"How do you know? You didn't really give him a chance. From what you said, you were great together, and he wanted to spend more time with you. But at some lunch, he was being nice to this girl, and you flipped out."

"She was an idiot," I told him.

"And you thought so little of Ronnie that you figured he'd rather be with someone like that than with you. Boy, I thought I raised a man with half a brain. So she was flirting with him. So what? The two of you are figuring things out, or you were. But instead of seeing where things could go, you got scared off by an airheaded Barbie doll. Doesn't sound like you, does it?"

"Yeah, it does, Dad. I'm too old to play those games. What I think I really want is someone to come home to, go to sleep with every night, and who'll still be there in the morning. Oh, and someone to really shake the bed with."

Dad rolled his eyes. "Then get a damn Saint Bernard. You want more than that, and you know it. Brian was safe and dull as dirt. Before you die, go for the excitement, the ol' brass ring. If you get your heart broken, it will heal. But I can tell you this from experience: playing it safe only leaves you old and alone in the end, wondering what the hell happened to all those dreams you had."

"Do you really have a lot of regrets?"

"About your mother? No. But I wish I'd stayed in college. I enrolled, but it was difficult, and then we had you and we needed money and your mom needed help, so I let life take over. There are plenty of things I would do again, and some things I'd change, and that's one of them." Dad began to get up. I'd finished eating so I took care of the dishes. Dad got around pretty well with his walker, and by the time I was done cleaning up, he was back from the bathroom and in his usual spot, engrossed in the television.

I sat on the sofa and wondered if Dad was right. Had I given up on Ronnie too soon? I'd never know. That bridge had been burned, I was sure. "Do you need anything, Dad?"

"Just for you to stop moping around here," he retorted.

"I'm keeping you company for a while." I turned to the television, but I wasn't interested in what Dad was watching, so I got busy around the condo until it was time for Dad to go to bed. I stayed up, unable to sleep, watching crap on television until I couldn't stay awake any longer.

In the morning I made Dad breakfast and then left, driving home once again. I kept hoping that I'd get one of the texts or calls that I'd gotten from Ronnie every weekend, but like the rest of the week, the phone remained eerily quiet. Not that I expected anything else, but it only reinforced my loneliness and stupidity.

Since I was early enough getting back into town, I went right to the gym. The guys were still there, and they all waved or nodded. Ronnie was busy with a set. I returned the greeting and hurried to the locker room to change. When I was dressed, I wanted to join them to talk and see what was going on, but I wasn't sure I was welcome. I had spent much of my life on the outside looking in, and I was doing it all over again.

I got on a treadmill and got the machine started. After a few minutes, Phillip came up and took the machine next to me.

"Okay, spill it, what's going on?" he said as he started walking. "Ronnie is being really quiet, and you're not working out with us. What did we do?"

"Nothing. You guys haven't done anything," I told him.

"Is it Ronnie?" he asked.

I tried my best not to react. Lying wasn't something I did well.

"What happened between you?" I had turned away, but when I looked back at Phillip, he gasped loudly. "No way."

"You're drawing your own conclusions," I told him.

"You and Ronnie?" Phillip giggled and covered his mouth. "How? When? I knew he was really open-minded, but he's into girls," he stage-whispered.

I shook my head. "I'm not talking about this, and you need to forget everything you think you know." I wasn't going to start rumors about Ronnie. That wasn't fair. "And if you repeat anything, I'll start a rumor that you're into... I don't know... golden showers or something."

Phillip curled his lip and then made a buttoning motion, which lasted all of two seconds. "At least that explains why he's been weird all week."

"A world record for keeping quiet, I see."

"Come on. This is too exciting not to at least ask about. So was it good?"

"Phillip. I'm not going to talk about it, and whatever happened doesn't matter because it's over. Ronnie will have moved on."

"Nope," Phillip said with a grin. "We were out the other night, and this waitress with huge boobs practically had them in his face, and he placed his order and continued talking to us. When Jerry asked him what was wrong with him, Ronnie practically bit his head off. It was like after he and Maggie split, except he isn't talking about it at all. He's just cranky."

"The thing is that I screwed things up, and I don't know how to fix it." I turned to where Ronnie lay on one of the flat benches, pressing dumbbells. I could see his chest muscles extend and clench as he worked. Even from a distance it was sexy. "I don't know if I can fix it."

Phillip nodded. "That's not what he said."

"Huh?"

"When I asked him what was wrong, he didn't say anything other than that he had messed something up."

I hit the Pause button on the machine. "He said that?"

"Yeah. Do you want me to do something to help?"

I turned away and stared once again out over the gym floor. "No." There was nothing Phillip could do. Whatever happened now was up to Ronnie and me. I hoped like hell one of us had the guts to make the first move. I restarted the machine and began walking again, hoping the exercise would give me the courage to eat a lot of crow.

I BEGGED off lunch with the guys and went home after the gym. The ten minutes I was in the sauna with Ronnie told me that was best. The mixture of heat and sweat with a side of tension was too much, and I figured a meal would be just as tense, so I got some takeout on the way home, effectively undoing any good I'd done at the gym, and sat in front of the television to eat. I called my dad and a few friends who I hadn't seen in a while—none of whom were home—and ended up just going to bed for a little quiet time. I hadn't realized until the past week just how important Ronnie and the guys were to me. I needed to make new friends. But a hell of a lot of good that realization was going to do me at the moment.

After taking a short nap, I went outside to work in the yard. It was hot, and I watered the plants and then sat on one of the loungers in the shade, wishing I had brought a book and some tea. So with a groan, I went back and got them.

"You know you can be a huge pain in the ass," Ronnie said when I came back outside. He stood next to my lounger, staring at me with his hands on his hips.

"That makes two of us," I told him, putting down my glass. "You want one?" There was no reason to be inhospitable, and I hurried inside, grabbing a glass and the pitcher from the refrigerator. When I came back out, Ronnie was sprawled out on my lounger, and I sat in the chair, putting my feet up on the stool. I handed him the glass, and he poured what he wanted of the tea.

We sat like that for ten minutes, the only sound the clinking of the ice cubes in the glasses. "We're quite a pair, aren't we?"

"Hell yes," Ronnie agreed. He sat up. "I don't know what the hell is supposed to happen now, but I came here to tell you something, and I'm going to do that."

"Okay."

He'd had the guts to come see me; the least I could do was listen to him.

"Sometimes you're a total pain in the ass."

"I think you already said that."

"Yeah, but it bears repeating until it sinks into your head. You're a smart guy, and you take care of everyone else. But sometimes you think that means you know what everyone else is thinking and what they want. Let me tell you something... you don't!"

"Is that what you came here to say?" I drank the rest of my tea. "Because if it is, it's hot out here and I'm going to go inside." I stood.

"Bullshit! Sit back down and listen till I'm done. You did a lot of talking the other day, and now it's my turn." I sat. "Sometimes you're so sanctimonious."

"You've said that too. Maybe you should broaden your vocabulary."

He leaned closer. "Maybe I should drop my pants and slip my cock between your lips so I can get a word in." That shut me up and made my mouth water at the same time. "You made it clear that you called things off because you thought it was what I wanted, which is bullshit. I think you were scared."

"Of course I was," I admitted. "You are, for most intents and purposes, straight. Or whatever label you want to put on yourself. You've been with women your whole life."

"And now, because of you, I discovered this part of myself that I never knew. And I want to explore it… with you, dumbass. If you want to know if this is going to work between us, I don't know. If you want an assurance that I won't want a woman in my life again, then all I can tell you is that I don't know. But I can say that I will never cheat on you behind your back. And if my feelings should change, I will certainly tell you."

"You make this sound like one of your deals," I said.

"Those were just the formalities, because I don't know what's going to happen." He touched my lips, and the forming words died. "I've loved you for a long time. You've been my best friend for a while now. I won't ever knowingly hurt you, and what's between us is more than sex. You touched my heart that first night. And you've held it since. I had no intention of going home with Monica or any of the girls who approached me this past week. Because none of them are you."

"Oh." I felt like a complete fool.

"Yeah. So I don't know what to do from here."

"What would you do with anyone else you were dating? Yes, I'm a guy, but things aren't really that different."

Ronnie reached into his pocket and pulled out a watch. "This is the one I used to wear."

There was no way I could take it. I'd admired that gold Rolex when Ronnie had worn it. "No. Put that back in your pocket. I don't want gifts from you. At least not that kind. What I want from you is your time and attention." I pressed the watch back into his hand.

"You know I'm very busy."

"Yeah, but think about it—all anyone wants is to be cared for. That's all anyone wants. I don't want money or gifts. I have a job of my own and can buy whatever I want." I pointed to the lounger, and he reclined again.

"So...."

"So we make plans and you stick to them. If we have something planned, that doesn't mean that the guys or clients are invited to come along. I don't expect you to stop seeing your friends or not go out with clients—that's part of your job—but don't blow me off and think you can say you're sorry with gifts." He'd done that with Maggie all the time, and while I wasn't going to bring her up by name, I wanted him to remember that. "Just being yourself is enough." I got up and walked over to the lounger, straddling it. "You know this isn't going to be easy."

"I know, and this isn't some magic conversation that makes everything all better," Ronnie said.

I nodded slowly. "No, it isn't."

Ronnie reached for me, cupping my cheeks and guiding my face closer to his. "How about we go inside?"

I kissed him, but then I shook my head. "Not today."

"Why?" he asked with a sly smile. "You have something important to do besides lying outside in the backyard?"

I leaned closer, inhaling his scent, and it went right to my groin. He smelled good, and in his tight shirt that hugged his arms just right he looked like a million bucks. "We've been friends for years, and then we stumbled into having sex. I don't want to stumble anymore. It's Saturday, and I have things I need to do. So do you. Tomorrow we'll meet, go to the gym, and afterward we'll have lunch and spend the afternoon together. It'll be a date day. Is that okay?"

He lightly stroked up my hands and over my ass. "You want to make me wait until then?" He was playing, and my pants got tighter by the second.

"Yes. See, I love that you came over here today. You made me feel on top of the world just by being here, and I want you to feel like that too. So I'm not going to rush, and I'll try not to push you." I was still nervous as hell about the whole "dirty little secret" thing, but my dad had been right, and I needed to give him a chance. "So do we have a date for tomorrow?"

"You bet." He grinned and I kissed him. He started and pulled away when he heard voices approaching behind the hedge.

Slowly, I moved back to my chair and tried not to let the disappointment show. I had to remind myself that it had taken me some time to get used to the idea of being different, and I needed to give Ronnie that same time. It still bothered me a great deal. I had been out for a long time and wasn't prepared to go back into the closet.

"Hey, it'll be okay." Ronnie told me, and I chose to believe it for now. He stood and hugged me. "I mean it. I know you're scared, and I've about pissed myself more than once over this whole thing, but I'm here."

I returned the hug, then released him. "I'll see you tomorrow."

Ronnie looked confused, but he said good-bye and left the yard. I heard his car roar to life, then he peeled rubber and the engine quieted. Then it got louder. I walked to the street. Ronnie cruised by slowly, window down, grinning at me. "Just wanted to see you before tomorrow." He never actually stopped, but he didn't have to. I smiled and watched the slate-black Lamborghini slide by and then speed up before the rumble once again faded into the distance.

I wanted to jump up and down. Honestly I didn't think I felt the ground under my feet as I walked back to the house. I pulled out my phone with a grin.

Thanks, Dad, I texted.

For what?

Just being you.

I got a smiley face in return. I put the phone away and slid down into my chaise lounge, looking up at the sky through quivering greenery overhead. There was still a lot to work out, but try as I might, the smile on my face didn't dim for at least an hour.

OF COURSE by the next morning the doubts and worries had kicked in again, and I was wondering if Ronnie would follow through on what he'd said. We met for breakfast before going to the gym, and I kept expecting him to explain that something had come up or that he'd promised to go to lunch with a client, or God knows what, but nothing.

"Work things out?" Phillip asked once we were alone. I tried not to smile, I really did, but I couldn't help it.

"I don't know. We talked and things are... still weird, but maybe a little less so."

Phillip shook his head as we walked across the gym floor. "You know, if this works out, the entire gym-bunny population is going to want to scratch your eyes out." He grinned for a second and then got serious. "You know it's true. They all have their eyes on him... or at least his big... car." Phillip giggled like an eight-year-old.

"They'll get over it," I said quietly. I wondered if Ronnie would. I could hear the same voice in my head that was there in the restaurant. I wanted it quiet, but the damn thing wouldn't shut the hell up.

"Of course they will." Phillip practically ran up the stairs to the cardio equipment, and we found treadmills close to each other and started them up. "I know I tease you, but I'm jealous as hell in one way. I don't envy you in another, though." And I knew exactly what he meant. I probably shouldn't have, but I did. "Ronnie is really hot, but he has a lot of baggage, and that's with women."

"I think I help with some of that," I said quietly.

I expected a chuckle or another joke, but his expression became serious. "I know you do. You always have. Like with the baseball cards. The guys will go along with whatever Ronnie says because, well... he has a lot of money, and frankly they're all hoping he'll spend some of it on them. You don't expect that or care about it. You listen and don't take much of his bullshit, and I think that's what he needs. Most women won't do that. Maggie did for a while, but Ronnie wore her out, and in the end it got easier for her to go along than to fight him. At least that's what she said once."

"I knew before that. The sparkle that was there for a long time after they met was gone, and she seemed tired and wrapped up in other things. People should have their own interests, and that's good, but they weren't interested in each other anymore." I had seen it, and I was using that as a model of what not to do. "Don't say anything to Ronnie about any of this. I promised I wouldn't talk about it." But I had to speak to someone—if only to keep my sanity—and Phillip was certain to understand.

"Of course not." Phillip returned his attention to his workout, and I opened my book, but I didn't read much. My attention kept getting pulled to where Ronnie was. "You got it bad," Phillip said after a while. "Do you think he'll come out?"

That was the big question. "I need to give him time," I answered, ducking the question because I really didn't know. "You and I have known we were gay for a long time and have had a chance to deal with it. He's discovered a new part of himself and deserves that same chance."

Phillip didn't seem to be buying it. He rolled his eyes and then turned away. "I think it's a crapshoot, if you want my opinion."

I didn't, but I knew he was right. It was the one topic I hated thinking about in regard to all this. Ronnie had made me some promises, and until he proved otherwise, I was going to believe them. I sighed and forced my attention to my book. This was getting me nowhere, other than more and more nerved up. Instead of thinking about it, I delved into the book, and when that proved impossible, I thought about the fact that Ronnie and I were going to lunch and would have the afternoon together.

Once my workout was done, I headed into the locker room. I kept expecting Ronnie to say there had been a change of plans, but after the sauna, whirlpool, and showers, he met me by the front door.

"Where are we going?" I asked.

"Just go to my place," he said and we left.

I got there first. When Ronnie arrived, he opened the garage and motioned for me to park my car inside. I did, but it didn't bode well. He wanted my car out of sight. I got out and slowly walked to where Ronnie waited, his sports car purring. Ronnie's door lifted and he got out, motioning me to take his seat. "Go ahead."

"You want me to drive?" I asked as I slid behind the wheel of a car that cost about what I made in three years.

"Of course. You need to know how to drive it because what's mine is yours."

"I like my car."

"I know. But just so you know—" We pulled the doors closed, and he turned to smile at me. "—you look good." He meant in the car, but I smiled anyway.

"So do you," I whispered. Hell, he looked amazing in his tight white shirt that hugged his chest and arms perfectly. I put the car in gear and slowly backed out. There was amazing power in the car, and the difficult part was keeping it under control. This was a car built for speed and performance as well as for show and design.

"Watch where you're going," Ronnie said lightly when I turned to him as we pulled to a stop at a light.

"I'd so much rather look at you."

Ronnie's eyes softened, and I saw him look at me the way I'd always wanted to be looked at. Brian had loved me, but he'd never adored me. Ronnie's gaze said I was the center of the world, and I wasn't sure how to handle it or whether to believe it. Not that his gaze was lying, but I must have been seeing things.

"Continue on and the road will take you to Duke's."

"Okay." On a Sunday the place would be jumping. They had a huge deck that would be packed with people. When we arrived, Ronnie told me to go past, turn around, and pull up to the door. When I did, we were waved into a space right in front. I guess in one of these, finding a parking space was never a problem.

We got out and went inside, where we were shown directly to a table at the edge of the shade by the river. I sat down, and Ronnie took one of the chairs in the sun. He tanned beautifully and never burned, unlike me.

"Did you have a good workout?" I asked. God, I didn't know what in the hell to talk about. In all the time we'd been friends, I'd never had that problem.

"Great. How is your dad?" Ronnie asked.

"Doing better," I answered, and then things grew quiet and we picked up the menus. "This sucks."

"What, the restaurant? We can go wherever you like," Ronnie said.

"No." I set down my menu. "I've known you for years, and you always have tons to talk about. But we're sitting here staring at each other."

"I guess it's because I've never been on a date with a guy before," he whispered.

"What do you talk about on your other dates?" I asked.

"What we're going to do when we get done eating," he answered.

The waiter approached, and I caught his eye. The kid blanched a little and veered off toward another table. I turned back to Ronnie. "You mean like when we get to your place, I'm going to strip you bare, lick and suck every inch of you until you forget your own name, and then, when you're begging me to let you come, I'm going to slide my cock in you and ride you until you scream loudly enough that half the town can hear you? Because that's only the beginning. I know you're hard right now—so am I—but no squirming, and don't think of going to the bathroom to take care of things. I want you so damn hot you can't see straight." I grinned.

Ronnie swallowed. "Are you going to suck my cock?"

"Until your head melts, and then I'm going to slide my cock between your plump lips and give you the education of a lifetime. Whenever you suck me just right, I'll rub my finger on that spot you love so much, and I'm going to send you to the moon." Ronnie's eyes had practically crossed, and I doubted he could actually read the menu.

"I'm not so sure about...."

I leaned really close once again. "You know how it feels when I suck you?" Ronnie gasped and nodded quickly. "Don't you want me to feel that too?"

"Fuck yeah, I do," he said with determination, and then he smiled.

"And believe me, I'll make it worth your while. Besides, I have a feeling you're going to love it." I grinned and sat back in my seat.

The server approached again. Ronnie ordered ice tea with a little cranberry, and I had diet soda. "Then, this afternoon, when the house is really quiet and maybe after a nap, I'm going to roll you on your belly, massage your back until you're nice and loose, slip my cock inside you, and massage you on the inside as I rub your back. You aren't going to make a sound, not even when you shoot the load of your life."

Ronnie swallowed hard, and when the drinks came, he gulped from his glass.

"You're so hard right now you can't stand it," I whispered, because I sure as hell was. "Do you want me to make you come right here at the table?"

"Where everyone can see?" he asked. I knew that got him hot. "They know me here."

"I won't touch you and you won't touch yourself, but I can make you come right here right now. Just think about the way your cock is jumping in your pants right now. The jeans you're wearing, rough on your skin, feel perfect, tight, gripping you, rubbing you just the way you like it. I could run my fingers along your cock, teasing the head and the spot just below, the way I do with my tongue that makes you want to howl. You're seconds away from coming right now, aren't you?"

"Yeah…," Ronnie whimpered, and I grew quiet. "Clay."

"Oh, you aren't going to come yet. I want you to know what's on the menu next, the real important menu."

"You fucker," Ronnie swore half under his breath.

I saw the waiter approaching again. "Do you really want to come now, or let it build?" Ronnie called me a name, and I smiled, turned to the waiter, and placed my order.

We both got salads because we were being good, though I did get the naughty ranch dressing because I loved the stuff. "So how is work?" I asked, figuring it would be a good idea to change the subject.

"The market is up and people have money they want to give me right and left. This job is counterintuitive, I think you know that.

151

The money dries up and sits on the sidelines when times are tough and floods in when the market is going well. The thing is that it's the clients I get during lean times who make the most money because they buy low and wait for the markets to rebound." He grinned and sat back as though he'd unlocked the secret of the universe. He was so cute like that. "That's what you did, and your retirement is up by half in four years."

"I know. It's because you're brilliant with money." He puffed out his chest a little. "Don't get a big head or anything else." I rolled my eyes, and he puffed up more. "Stop that."

"It's my turn to get you hot," Ronnie whispered.

"You've always been able to do that," I admitted. I glanced down at the table. "I wonder what you see in me sometimes." Ronnie didn't say anything, and I raised my gaze. "You have to know that, guys or girls, you can get pretty much anyone you want."

Ronnie nodded and then broke into a grin. "I know."

"Smartass."

"There's a difference between being able to do something and actually doing it. And yeah, now that I know what it's like to be with a guy, I wonder what it would be like to be with…." He glanced around. "The guy in the corner with the guns of steel."

"Thanks."

"But then I think he's huge, probably vain, most likely spends all his time either at the gym or talking about his muscles, and thinks the height of class is a burping contest."

"You've had those," I told him.

"And I always win, but that's bar behavior, and as you said once, I'm not living in a frat house anymore." Ronnie leaned close. "He goes to the gym, and he's juiced so much…."

"So you like me for my big dick," I said.

Ronnie instantly got serious. "I like you," he told me, his gaze searingly hot. "I know I have a huge mouth and shoot it off a lot. Most of that is for attention and effect. You know that and call me on it. But I'm being honest. I wouldn't be with another man because I don't trust any other man the way I trust you."

Holy crap, that about said it all. It didn't deal with women, though, and I had to give that time and see where it fell. I didn't know what to say. It had been so unexpected. "Ummm...."

"You trust me too, right?" he asked.

"Yes." The thing was, I did, and that answered a lot of the questions and concerns that had been plaguing me. I did trust him, and that was where everything had to be built. I trusted that he wasn't going to break my heart on a whim. Sometimes it happened. Brian said that wasn't his intention when he left, just that things between us had run their course. Maybe he was right, because the excitement and sheer joy of being with Ronnie outshone anything that I'd had with Brian. Brian was high maintenance....

"What are you smiling about?" Ronnie asked.

"I was thinking about Brian. He was so high maintenance and dammit if you aren't too, but in a different way." I took a bite of salad.

"Brian was a prima donna pain in the ass. If everything wasn't exactly the way he liked it, he made things miserable for everyone else. He was loud—"

"That's the pot calling the kettle black," I teased.

"Maybe. But he wasn't a lot of fun to be around, and you weren't when you were with him. I'm way more fun than him."

"Maybe," I said with a smile. "You do have some advantages."

"I'm hotter than he was."

"No doubt." And Ronnie was up for anything, anytime in the bedroom. That was a major turn-on. "But you know you have your own idiosyncrasies."

Ronnie nodded. "I'm high maintenance, no doubt about it. But maybe I'm your kind of high maintenance." He took a drink of his tea.

"You belch and you're wearing that drink," I said flatly. I knew what was coming. He swallowed and put his glass down. "Manners count, and they say a lot about how much you care about the person you're with. If you act like a frat boy around me, then that says you see me as a frat brother. If you act like someone who cares about what I think and behaves properly, then that says you care about my opinion and want others to see how much you think of me." I took another bite and swallowed. "Why do you think I'm always polite even when you and the guys are acting like children? Because I care, and the company you keep reflects on you. So I've always been nice to your mother and pleasant when you brought clients along with us. They weren't my clients, but my behavior reflected on you."

Ronnie stared at me, openmouthed, and blinked a few times. He placed his fork on the plate and wiped his mouth. "Jesus.... That explains a hell of a lot." He didn't go into any more at that moment, but I figured I'd said more than enough.

"I didn't mean to be insulting, and if I got on my high horse, I'm sorry, but you see how I can be high maintenance too. I've had people treat me like crap, and I'm too old to take it any longer, especially from someone I care about."

Ronnie nodded. "Is that what you meant yesterday?"

"Have you ever watched the movie *My Fair Lady*?" I shook my head as soon as the question passed my lips, and Ronnie rolled his eyes and gave me one of those "are you nuts?" looks. "To make a long story short, it's about a professor and a flower girl. He teaches her how to speak so they can pass her off in society. I won't go into it, but the important point is that at one point Eliza says that the difference between a flower girl and a duchess isn't how she acts but how she's treated. And I want to be treated like a duchess. Not with presents, but in the way you behave around me."

"But what about you?"

I stared at him. "Have I ever treated you in any way other than as a prince? Think about it."

"Son of a bitch," Ronnie swore a little too loudly, and the people at the next table looked over briefly and then turned back to their food.

"Don't swear or I'll have to punish you when we get home." I deepened my voice, and Ronnie stilled and swallowed. "I'm kidding."

"You had me scared."

"I'll never knowingly hurt you. I can promise you that." I grinned and continued eating. It was hot, and the server brought more drinks, which I finished quickly. The humidity was through the roof, and by the time we were done eating, I swear I'd sweated out everything I'd drunk. Ronnie got the check, and we got up to leave. I followed him out of the restaurant and to the car. He had me drive home, and I had to admit, I could get used to driving that car. It was amazing. He had me park in the drive, then got out and went right inside the house. I wondered what his hurry was, but I found out as soon as I closed the door.

He pushed me against it, and I grinned. God, it was heady being wanted this badly, and for me it had been a very long time.

"No," I whispered to Ronnie when I saw him reaching to pull off his shirt. "I will undress you. You can take off your shoes and socks. Nothing more." I pulled him to me, kissing him hard. I wanted him more than I'd ever wanted anyone, even the guys I used to dream about when I was a teenager.

Ronnie tugged at my shirt, and I let him pull it over my head. He was usually reticent when it came to touching or kissing me, but I groaned long and low when he looked at me and then licked one of my nipples before sucking it until it was hard and I was aching.

"How did you know how to do that?" I asked.

"I did what you do to me sometimes," Ronnie whispered.

I unfastened my pants, let them pool around my ankles, and closed my eyes, waiting to see what Ronnie would do. He stilled and I could feel the war within him. Then he trailed his fingers down my chest and over my briefs. I said nothing and didn't move. This had to be his decision. If he was never going to be comfortable touching me, then....

Ronnie pushed my briefs down my legs, and I gasped when he stroked me. "Like that?"

"Don't you?" I asked.

"Fuck yeah."

"Then why wouldn't I? That's the beauty of being with a guy—we basically like the same things. There's no wondering if you're doing it right—guys will always tell you." I kept my eyes closed, but Ronnie released me. Then a few seconds later, hot lips slid down me. "God," I breathed and kept my hips still. "That's it, baby. Take what you can but don't rush. Do what you like."

I slapped my hands on the door as he circled his tongue around the base of the head and then at the spot underneath. Holy hell that was good. "Damn, you're good." Oral sex wasn't usually my thing, but he felt amazing, and that was all because of how special he was. I pushed back on the door and breathed steadily.

After a few minutes, I opened my eyes and leaned forward, pulling him up. "Come on," I whispered. I pulled up my pants and took his hand, leading him to the bedroom and shutting the door.

I pushed Ronnie toward the bed and got out of my clothes, walking naked toward him. I grabbed his shirt and tugged it over his head. "You are gorgeous." I pressed him back on the bed, his legs hanging off the edge, feet still on the floor. "You know I could make you come right now."

"You could?"

"Oh yeah. You remember at the restaurant? I can make you come in your pants." I lifted his legs and spread them, running my hands up his jeans-clad thighs. "But I don't want that. I want you to come with me deep inside you, stroking your big cock until you can't hold back anymore." I unfastened his jeans, easing the stretch of the denim down his legs. Then I pressed his knees to his chest and tugged on the fabric, baring his ass. Fuck, that sight was something else. I was hard as hell, and all I wanted was to spread his cheeks farther and take him. But I restrained myself. Rushing would cause pain, and I wanted none of that. "Keep your legs there," I told him, stepping back and burying my face between his cheeks, licking and sucking at his opening.

"Fuck yeah...." His groaning pushed me, adding intensity, driving my own passion. The taste of musk and man filled my mouth. I paused and tugged off his pants, tossing them to the floor, then worked my thumb inside him, twisting and pumping while I sucked his cock. I knew exactly what drove Ronnie wild, and this was damn near it. I wasn't ready to give him everything, but within minutes he was on the edge.

"Clay, I need it."

"I know. You're right on the edge," I whispered, pumping his cock and doing just enough to keep him there. "And that's right where I want you." I wiggled my thumb, and his eyes rolled. "Are you ready for me to fuck you?"

"Damn…," he breathed.

"Then reach and get a condom."

He stretched to the nightstand and handed me one, along with the bottle of lube. I slicked my fingers and pulled away my thumb, then slid two long fingers deep into him. Then I pulled out, leaving him empty. I tore open the package and rolled on the condom with shaking hands. I wasn't going to last for very long at this rate, but I didn't care. Ronnie wasn't going to last either. He was way too worked up, and that was exactly how I wanted him.

Ronnie's groans filled the room as I slid into him, filling him, his heat gripping me, pulling me deeper. When my hips pressed to Ronnie's ass, I gripped his cock tight, but I didn't move my hand. I could feel the blood coursing through him. I pulled back and away before driving into him.

"Holy fuck!"

"Yeah," I groaned as I did it again, sending ripples through him. "I've loved you for a long time. You're my best friend and more. I've seen you many ways, but I like you best just like this." I pressed into him one more time and held still. "I want to see you like this all the time—smiling, out of your head with passion. You want me so badly right now you can't think, and I want you more than I've wanted anyone in my life." I leaned forward, kissing him hard. "I love you, Ronnie."

I didn't expect him to say it back, and in fact I wasn't looking for words from him. Ronnie dealt with words. I'd heard him say "I love you, man" at the end of phone conversations all the time. So before he could say anything, I bent my knees slightly, angling my cock just right so it would drag over that spot when I fucked him. Ronnie gripped the bedding. I still held him tight without stroking, and Ronnie did his best to flex his hips, trying for friction.

"I'm not going to stroke you." Instead, I squeezed and released my fingers. I knew it was only adding to his frustration, but that was the point. "And I know I'm driving you crazy." I leaned over him, gazing deep into his eyes. Depending on his behavior, sometimes they were full-of-shit brown, but right now, they were milk chocolate, glossy and smooth. "I want you to come for me. I don't need to stroke you."

"Yes, you do," Ronnie gasped.

"No, I don't. You want me so badly I can feel it. Your mouth is hanging open, and there's so much tension in your body you're afraid you're going to fly apart. I want you to come. Think about my hand touching you and my cock deep inside, filling you, rubbing that spot that drives you insane. That's all you want and need."

"It isn't. I...."

"I know what you think, but give yourself over to me. Let me have control and stop fighting me. As soon as you do you'll see I'm right and your balls will tingle, all those thoughts in your head will quiet, and it'll be just me and you. That's all that matters. Just me and you." I snapped my hips, and he gasped. I moved faster, listening to his moans get higher and more frantic.

"I can't," he begged, hands shaking.

"Oh yes, you can. You can do it for me. Show me what I mean to you and how I make you feel. Come for me now. I want to see you." I squeezed his cock tightly.

Ronnie gasped and held his breath before opening his mouth, whimpering softly, and then shaking like a leaf as his release poured out of him, painting his chest and belly. The sight was breathtaking. Ronnie in the throes of climax was indescribable. His eyes widened and shone, and his mouth hung open as though he couldn't believe this was happening to him. His muscles gripped me tight, and within seconds I followed him, throwing my head back and howling at the top of my lungs.

I couldn't move. I tingled from head to toe, and I was afraid to open my eyes in case the magic that surrounded me came to an end. I never wanted it to, but eventually my head cleared and I became aware of Ronnie still breathing heavily. I released his cock and slowly pulled out of him, missing the heat and pressure immediately. "You were made for me. Did you know that?"

"Huh?" Ronnie said.

"I'll explain later."

"No." He stroked my cheek. "Tell me."

"You always said your mom and dad were perfect together."

"Yeah. Mom said he was her 'once in a lifetime.'"

"I think you're mine. You were made for me whether you know it or not." I could feel it in a way I never had with Brian. When I was with him, love had grown slowly, but I didn't think it was deep enough. We got comfortable with each other, and we were happy enough, but it wasn't a grand passion. Even at the beginning. It wasn't like being with Ronnie.

I lay on the bed next to him, inhaling deeply. I tied off the condom and dropped it in the trash next to the bed. I figured I'd get a cloth when I could move. Ronnie did it instead. I heard him in the bathroom, washing, and then he brought out a cloth and towel for me. I used them, thanked him, and then pulled him down for a kiss that I wanted him to feel to his toes. He threw the used towel and cloth into the bathroom and climbed into bed.

"I asked my mom about when I was a kid. You know, what I told you about? She says there was a time when I had headaches and had hit my head, but she figured I'd been playing and fell. She told me she took me to the doctor. I don't remember that."

"You were young. Did you tell her anything more?" I tugged him until he rolled onto his side, and I cradled his head in my arms, stroking his hair.

"No. What good would it do? And it would only upset her over something she can't do anything about."

"Are you okay with what you remember? Can you process it and deal with it?" I asked. "That's what really counts."

"You know, I think I can." He smiled and kissed me. "I thought a lot about what you said, and I think you're right. I don't think he raped me. He may have intended to, but he didn't."

I believed that was likely as well, but another thought crept into my head. Concussions and brain injuries could affect the makeup of the brain. It had been in the news a lot with regard to the NFL. I wondered if Ronnie's obsessive-compulsive behavior was the result of that incident all those years ago. Of course I'd never know, and I kept that thought to myself because it didn't matter. Ronnie was Ronnie. It was my pleasurable job to love him.

"You're quite a man, you know. Most people wouldn't be able to keep that to themselves."

"It's not her fault, and I'm not going to hurt her over it now. I doubt I would have done that a few months ago."

"Oh...."

"Yeah. I would have told her, and then there would have been a huge dramatic scene because Mom would ask why I hadn't told her, and then I'd explain that it came to me while we were fucking, and then she'd scoff because who can remember anything during great sex.... It just isn't worth it." It almost seemed like a comedy routine. "It isn't going to change who I am."

"Good. I like who you are." The air-conditioning kicked on, and I lay still, listening to the soft hum. "What are we going to do for the rest of the afternoon?"

"Take a nap, fuck again, rinse, repeat." I chuckled and closed my eyes. Between the workout and the sex, I was ready for a few minutes of rest. I closed my eyes and dozed off. When I woke, Ronnie was asleep next to me, the sheet pooled around his waist. I smiled and pulled it away. He was soft, but a few strokes of my fingers had him half hard and well on the way to more, which I accomplished by sucking him hard.

"Fuck, what a way to wake up."

I sucked him until he was nearly ready to "bust a nut." Then I slid inside him again and slowly fucked him until he screamed to high heaven. We watched television after that, dozing in bed off and on until his phone rang. I groaned and threatened to slap him if he answered it. He did anyway, and I smacked his ass.

"Yeah, four is fine," Ronnie said. I glared at him as he hung up. "The guys will be here at four," he told me. I checked the time—it was just after three. I pushed off the covers, got out of bed, and glared at him.

"I knew you'd do this," I told him, crossing my arms over my chest.

"Don't get everything in a twist. They aren't staying very long. Bobby wanted to borrow some stuff, and since they were all at the go-cart track, I couldn't tell them all to stay away. It would be rude." He was hedging about something, but I didn't really care. "Let's go clean up." He tugged me toward the bathroom and started the water.

I was still pissed, and that lasted until Ronnie had me inside the massive shower and pressed to my back as he rubbed my chest and belly with soapy hands.

"It's so different than feeling yourself. I mean, you feel good and strong, different from a woman."

"Is it better?"

"Not better, not worse, just different. I like it. We work hard to stay trim and to build muscle," Ronnie said.

I turned. "I know, and I like it." I stroked his chest. "But don't think this gets you off the hook for breaking your promise yesterday."

"It won't be long. I swear," he said as he pressed me back against the tile. "I'll make it up to you." He went down on his knees, and I began to see the attraction of a good blowjob. Damn, he had talent. Maybe it had been Brian's technique the whole time. Who knew… and who fucking cared.

My legs shook by the time I warned Ronnie I was close. He sucked me harder, and I lost it, coming down his throat. I hadn't expected that, but Ronnie had been full of surprises. I used the tile wall to remain upright. Ronnie turned off the water and then pushed open the shower door and grabbed the towels. I took mine and stepped out, my legs a little shaky.

"I expected you to... not be interested in... certain things."

Ronnie flipped the towel over his head to dry his back. "I'm interested in everything to do with you." He smiled, and I was at a loss. I had not been prepared for this, and while it was nice to hear, I wasn't sure it was real. But, God, I really hoped it was.

I hung up the towels when we were done, and we got dressed, picking up our clothes from throughout the house. Ronnie turned on the game, and we sat on the hated curvy sofa. He answered the door when the guys knocked and let them inside.

"So what's going on?" Jerry asked as he strode in. He and Ronnie hugged, and Jerry went right into the kitchen and returned with beers in hand. He offered me one, but I shook my head, wondering what the hell was going on. This didn't look like they were there to borrow something. They crowded onto the sofa, watching the game, and I got up and headed to the door.

"Wait," Ronnie said, catching my arm. I glared bullets at him. This told me where I really stood with him. The television went silent.

"Hey," all three of them said in unison.

Ronnie tossed the remote on the shelf near the television. "I didn't ask you here to watch the game." Ronnie turned to me, and I crossed my arms over my chest. That little piece of news didn't shock me. The excuse about wanting to borrow something was too flimsy.

"Then what's going on?" Phillip asked.

"Well, you guys are my closest friends. We see each other all the time and do things together, so I wanted to tell you that Clay and I are seeing each other."

I could have heard a pin drop for two seconds.

"That's great," Phillip said first. "How long?"

"Pretty much since his dad got sick," Ronnie answered.

"So you're gay now?" Jerry asked belligerently.

"Ronnie isn't gay. He's able to have a relationship with both men and women," I answered. "As you've seen firsthand."

"Then why not just pick another woman?" Jerry pressed. "You have tons of them throwing themselves at you all the time. Choose one of them." He sounded desperate.

Phillip smacked Jerry on the shoulder. "Pig."

"What?"

"I never figured you had a problem with me or Clay," Phillip said with a hard glare. "If Ronnie and Clay decide to date, it's none of our business." He stood and gave Ronnie a hug. "I'm jealous. If I'd known it was a possibility, I would have gone after you," Phillip teased, and I saw some of the tension leave Ronnie. I could also see it was a possibility that he'd lose Jerry as a friend.

"But I don't understand," Jerry continued, jumping to his feet. "How can you just decide you like guys now?"

"I found out something about myself: I like both. Clay and I have been good friends, but we discovered that there's more between us. It's what I want to do." He took my hand and gripped it tight. "I love him."

Jerry reached for his beer and gulped the entire thing. "I don't understand any of this."

"You don't have to," Ronnie told him sharply. "My life isn't for you to judge, and I don't have to explain my decisions to you. You guys are my friends, so I wanted to tell you about Clay and me. He's important in my life."

Bobby finally moved and extended his hand to Ronnie. "I think it's cool. You've been different the past few weeks. Well, last week you were a pain in the ass, but before that, you seemed happy again, and if that was because of Clay, then I say go for it."

Jerry gaped at him. "You're okay with this?"

"Why aren't you?" Bobby asked right back. "Whoever Ronnie decides to date doesn't affect you."

I watched for Jerry's reaction and knew the instant he decided. Ronnie had lost a friend. "It's bad enough that people ask me…. If

163

I hang around them all the time, people are going to think I'm gay." Jerry walked toward the front door in a huff.

"Poser," Phillip called as the door closed.

"I'm sorry, Ronnie," I said softly.

"Don't be," Ronnie said. He slipped his arm around my waist, squeezing tight. "I've lost friends before, and we'll make new ones."

"The guy's just a wannabe," Phillip said. "A real friend doesn't care about stuff like that." Phillip glanced at Bobby, then sat next to him and put an arm around his shoulder. "How about you? Ever think about exploring the dark side?" Phillip waited about two seconds before bursting into laughter, with Bobby following right behind. The tension had been broken, and I leaned slightly against Ronnie.

"You did this for me, didn't you?" I whispered.

"Yeah. I knew I needed to show you that I wasn't going to deny you or keep what we have hidden."

"Does your mom know?" Phillip asked.

"Yeah. She sort of walked in on us," I answered with a grin. "It was embarrassing."

"It was funny," Ronnie said and then proceeded to tell both of them the story. That was Ronnie. Very little in my life was going to be off-limits for one of his stories. I had little doubt of that.

"Dolores was very nice about it," I added at the end. I placed my lips right next to Ronnie's ear.

Bobby stood and gathered the bottles. "I think you and I need to go so these two can stop making cow eyes at each other. I hope you guys are happy, and I think you being a couple is great, but there isn't enough bleach in the world for me to unsee stuff." He and Phillip headed to the door, and suddenly Phillip began to laugh.

"What's so funny?" Ronnie asked.

"We all came in my car," Phillip answered and then turned to Bobby. "Maybe Jerry decided to walk." Phillip pulled open the door, and both of them said good-bye before closing it.

"I do love you," I whispered when the house was quiet again. "You didn't have to do that, but I love that you did."

"I'm not going to keep this a secret." Ronnie kissed me, and I felt his passion rising. "I know I say the words a lot, but I love you. You make me unbelievably happy." He sucked at the base of my neck, and I groaned. God, I loved that.

"So what are we going to do for the rest of the evening?"

"Fuck, nap, rinse, repeat," Ronnie said and pulled me toward the bedroom.

"I thought nap came first," I said.

We tumbled on the bed, our laughter lasting until Ronnie began pulling off my clothes.

"Fuck the nap—this time you come first," Ronnie said. "And from now on."

What more could I possibly ask for?

Epilogue

"I HATE winter," Ronnie groused as he came in the house through the garage, the bang of the door reverberating through the space.

"There's, what, half an inch of snow?" I asked, laughing. "It will be fine."

"We have people we're supposed to meet for dinner, and I don't want to go back out in this crap." He took off his coat, and I glared at him until he hung it up. Ronnie definitely needed a maid, and I had made it abundantly clear that I would not be filling that role. Not that he was particularly messy, just careless.

"It's fine. I'll drive, and you can sit back and relax." The snow didn't bother me in the least.

"But it's so cold."

"And when we get home, I'll warm you up." I pushed him down onto the living room sofa and pressed his legs apart, running my hands down his suit pants until I got to the hard bulge I was expecting. I unbuckled his belt and opened his pants, pulling them down past his hips and butt. His cock stood at full attention, bobbing slightly in anticipation.

"Suck me," Ronnie pleaded. "I spent the entire fucking day thinking about what you did last night, and I couldn't get up from my desk."

I licked up his length, and Ronnie gasped and then exhaled long and slow, like he'd been holding his breath for hours. Sometimes the pressure and tension were like that for him—the ups and downs of the market ensuring that Ronnie rode a daily financial roller coaster. I took him deep without playing, letting him release the stress of his day. He needed release, and I gripped him hard, sucking. I slicked a finger alongside his cock and pressed it inside him, touching the sensitive spot I knew so well. Ronnie's breathing became rapid and shallow, and he came. I swallowed everything he had and then let him slip from my mouth.

"Damn, you're good," he sighed and lay back to catch his breath. "What about you?"

"What I got is for later. So go on into the bedroom." I waited while he stood, and then I followed him. I closed the door behind him and watched as he stripped. "I got a present for you."

"You did?"

"Yes. It's for you to wear tonight at dinner." One thing I had found was that Ronnie could become bored sometimes and needed someone who could keep his attention. I had an imagination like no other, so I delighted in ways to keep him on his toes. I handed him a bag, and he looked inside and then back at me. "Lay down on your belly for me."

"Are you kidding?" he said, handing me back the bag.

"Nope." I pulled out the medium-sized butt plug and grabbed the lube. "This is going to remind you of me all night long. While we're eating and when you're talking business to people I don't know, you'll think of me and remember that it's my plug inside you, touching you, and then you'll look at me and smile. It's going to drive you crazy." I massaged my hand up and down his back and then down his butt to his inner thighs. He spread his legs, and I slowly and carefully slid the plug inside him, teasing and petting him while I did so. I tapped it a few times, and he grunted softly. He was beautiful like this, and all mine. I leaned forward and kissed his lower back. Then I moved away.

"What if I have to... you know," he asked as he rolled over.

I placed a small packet in his hand. "Then take it out, do what you need to, clean it, and put it back." I stepped closer, thankful I was fully dressed or I'd end up taking him right there. "After dinner, when we get home, I'm going to take it out and ride you until you can't move."

Ronnie walked a little funny as he began to pull on a pair of jeans.

"I suggest you wear underwear, as much as I love your cock and the fact that you're already half hard for me." I took him in hand and stroked a few times. "This is only for me, and I don't want anyone else seeing it." His days of dick selfies had ended a long time ago, but he needed a reminder occasionally. He opened one of his drawers and pulled out a pair of black briefs, put them on, and then dressed in jeans and a silk shirt.

"I love this," he said, petting the material.

"That's why I got it for you." It looked amazing on him, and the deep red color suited him. When he was dressed, I slid my arms around his neck. "I do love you so much."

He chuckled. "Me too. I used to think I had a good life, but with you I have a complete life." Ronnie got his shoes and put on one of his thick leather coats. I loved how badass he looked in them. "I want to ask you something before we leave. We've been together for more than six months, and we spend most of our time either here or at your house. I was wondering if you'd move in with me? I want to be with you all the time. I used to look forward to going out to dinners with clients and hanging out with the guys. I still like them, but what gets me through the day is that at the end of it, you're there."

"Ronnie…."

"I know. You're afraid if you move in here, then you'll be moving into my house and things will be like they were with Brian or how they were with Maggie. I know I screwed up with her, I see that now, and I know you don't like this place very much."

"It's nice, but there's no yard and it's a fancy condo-slash-house." I could never figure out what to call the thing. "It doesn't feel like a home to me."

"I know. So I thought if you moved in with me here, you could sell your place in the spring, and then we could start looking for a place of our own, together. Equal partners. Your house will sell fast, I know it, and then once we found a place, we could put this on the market."

I hadn't thought he would ever consider that. "You're serious?"

"Of course I am."

"There's an older couple I know—they're friends of mine—and they've been talking about selling. It's a great house—stone, with a nice yard and plenty of room for a grand office for you."

"So you'll consider it?" Ronnie looked into my eyes. I loved when he did that. There was no doubt or hesitation, just care and love, along with bone-deep happiness.

"Sure I would. As long as you let me decorate and that awful curvy-back sofa goes to a good home." He knew I hated that thing.

Ronnie chuckled. "Fine. You can decorate the house, as long as I have an office and the family room with a huge-ass television." I had found out that he'd bought the furniture in one shopping spree when he bought the house and hadn't changed anything since then. Few of the pieces were important to him.

"How about we do it together so we're both happy and make the house ours, an extension of us?" I stroked his rough cheek. "Let's go to dinner so we can come back here and celebrate." I kissed him again and then got my coat. We left by the garage, and we got in the Lamborghini that Ronnie wanted me to drive. The looks I got at work the first few times I'd driven it in had been priceless.

I carefully drove to the restaurant and parked, then got out and waited for Ronnie. We walked in together and found the group already seated. Ronnie greeted everyone, shaking hands and playing his role as host to the hilt. He was a master of the schmooze. Then he sat down slowly, and I kept my expression neutral. The waitress, a tall, stunning girl who filled out her top to damn near bursting, stopped by the table to ask what we'd like to drink. I saw her watching Ronnie, giving him extra attention.

Ronnie looked up from his menu, glanced at her, and then turned to me without a second's pause. "Clay, what would you like?" Ronnie held my gaze, seeing me, his eyes warm and loving. I knew in an instant—he only had eyes for me.

Stay tuned for an excerpt from

Stranded

Stranded: Book One

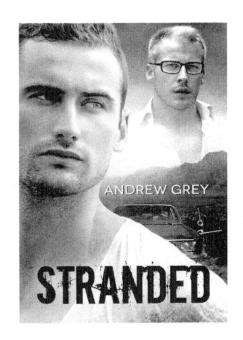

ANDREW GREY

STRANDED

Kendall Monroe is handcuffed to a car in the desert.

Is this life imitating art or art imitating life? The only thing he's sure of is that the situation he finds himself in is a copy of a scene he filmed earlier, only this time, there is no director yelling "cut" and no crew to rescue him. Terrified for his life, Kendall takes comfort remembering happier times with his longtime lover, Johnny. He hasn't seen Johnny in weeks since Johnny stayed behind to finish his latest best-selling novel.

As he attempts to survive scorching-hot days and freezing nights, Kendall tries to figure out who did this to him. Could it be Johnny, or the research assistant he suspects Johnny is having an affair with? Both options fill him with bitterness. Or is it a more likely suspect? Kendall has a stalker who sends him flowers and always seems to know where he is. But what does this stranger have to gain by leaving Kendall stranded in the middle of nowhere?

www.dreamspinnerpress.com

CHAPTER ONE

HE FIDGETED in his seat in the Dolby Theatre, gripping the armrest and holding his breath as the music sounded and the presenters walked out on stage, the starlet in an incredible gown that must have cost more than his parents' house, and the star in a tuxedo that actually shone a bit under the lights. They glided out to the podium and did their short shtick before getting to the business at hand. By this time, he figured his heart was two seconds from giving out. The man moved a tad closer to the microphone. "And the nominees for Best Actor are…."

A year or so earlier….

KENDALL MONROE rushed offstage and into the wings just after the lights faded. He had two minutes to change and get ready for his next entrance. He'd already pulled off his shirt, and his shoes had been kicked off, with one of the runners picking them up. He hurried behind a screen and shoved his pants down, then stepped out of them and into another pair already waiting. He was handed his shirt, and as soon as he walked out, the shirt was buttoned and his tie placed around his neck and tightened. His collar was fixed, and he shrugged on his coat. Shoes were already in front of him as if by magic, and he slipped them on. They were tied for him, and one of the wardrobe people gave him a good once-over, nodded, and Kendall walked back toward the wings to await his cue.

He stepped out of the wings and met his costar in the center of the stage, where they did their final scene together, she in his arms, and he guiding her through the final dance number. The music built, he kissed her, and then the stage opened up and the rest of the cast joined them, adding their voices to the stars' as the music, lyrics, and dance all built to a crescendo that ended with everyone taking their final pose and waiting for the curtain to drop.

As soon as the fabric hit the floor, Kendall breathed a sigh of relief. Everyone hurried off the stage, and the curtain rose again. Cast members rushed back out on stage for their bows, and at the very end, Kendall and Joyce held hands and walked back on stage. The applause grew, echoing thunderously off the walls of the theater. They bowed together, and then the rest of the cast came together around them. Kendall clasped hands with Jeffrey, like he always did in this choreographed display of fake spontaneity, bowed again, blew kisses to the audience, and then bowed one more time before stepping back and letting the curtain come down for the last time.

As soon as he walked offstage and down to his dressing room, it hit Kendall that this was the last time he'd play the handsome, dashing, and sometimes bumbling Stone. The run was over—not because they weren't selling tickets, but because the producers hadn't been smart enough to leave their options open when they'd negotiated with the theater, and another show was booked and ready to start rehearsals.

Kendall changed out of his final costume and into his street clothes. A knock sounded on his door. "Come in," Kendall called, and Joyce stepped inside.

"Can you believe we're actually closing?" she asked, flopping down on the sofa.

"No," Kendall said, sitting next to her. One of the things they'd discovered when they'd begun working together months ago was that neither of them wanted the crush of people that always seemed to appear after a show. So either she came to his dressing room or he went to hers, and they hid until things quieted down and they could leave in peace. Most of the others in the cast and crew respected their need for quiet and a chance to decompress. "Even my agent hasn't been looking very hard because he thought the producers would come up with a way for the show to continue. We've sold out for weeks, but there aren't any available theaters right now, so…."

"I know," she said. "I was really hoping this engagement would be extended for another few months."

"Have you heard any more about doing that reality show?" Kendall asked as he got up. He pulled a bottle out of the mini refrigerator and popped the cork. "I know we don't normally do this, but I thought we deserved to celebrate a bit." Kendall poured two glasses of the champagne and handed one to Joyce. "Here's to you," he said, raising his glass. "I've loved every day working with you."

"Me too," she said, and they clinked glasses. "I'm to start filming the Housewives of Massapequa in a few weeks." Joyce chuckled and then burped a little. "I never thought I'd do one of those shows, but I'm looking forward to it." She held up her hand. "I promise not to take the whole thing too seriously." Kendall sat back down and closed his eyes for a second as he let the bubbling wine slide down his throat. "I'm going to miss dancing with you eight shows a week." She sipped from her glass. "Do you realize you're the first partner I've had who's never stepped on my foot or given me bruises on my ankles?"

"You're kidding," Kendall said and downed the contents of his glass before pouring another. He topped hers off as well.

"Nope," she said with a grin. "You remember I was in Mamma Mia before this. I came home after each performance with a new bruise. My dance partner always figured my feet were part of the stage." She took another drink, and Kendall listened. There was still noise coming from outside, but the sounds were diminishing. Joyce finished her glass and then stood up. Kendall did the same and hugged her tight. "I'm going to miss you."

Kendall nodded. "Please call me and let me know how the show is going."

"And you be sure to let me know where you land," Joyce said, heading for the door. "I just know there's something great waiting just around the corner for you." They hugged again, and then she left.

"I certainly hope so," Kendall said to the empty room as a sort of prayer before gathering his things for the last time. He packed up everything he'd kept there for the run of the show. It took two bags but eventually he had it all, and once he was sure he'd left nothing behind, Kendall opened his door and stepped out in the hallway. He walked down to where he knew he'd be able to find the director. The producers were with him.

"Kendall," the producer who seemed to do all the talking said as he approached. He hadn't wanted to disturb them by interrupting their conversation. "We're all sorry about the way things worked out, and both Jerry and I hope to work with you again in the future. You brought life and fun and more depth to Stone than we thought possible."

"Thank you," Kendall said, shaking hands with Roger and Jerry before offering his hand to Gregory, the director. He accepted the envelope that would contain a statement of his final payment for the show; the check would go to his agent, Sal. After saying good-bye one more time, Kendall turned and left the theater. As soon as the stage door closed behind him, he turned and looked at it, having the strangest feeling that things were about to change in a big way.

He'd been working in Broadway theater for almost fifteen years, and he was a star. He'd risen from the chorus to small parts to understudy, and then finally to the lead of his first show, which had run for five years. After that, the theater world had been his oyster and he'd been able to pick his roles, just like he'd decided to do the role of Stone. But in this economy there weren't a lot of roles available, and for the first time, he wasn't able to move almost immediately from one role to another. Granted, it wasn't the money he was worried about. He'd lived fairly frugally, knowing that in theater there were ups and downs. He just hadn't expected the downs to come like this—a smash hit that ended before anyone expected it would.

Kendall took a final look at the nondescript door and then walked toward the sidewalk. The after-theater crowd was still out and about, heading to bars and restaurants before going home. Kendall had done the eating and partying after shows a few times, but his waist and pocketbook had paid the price, so he hadn't done that in a while. He'd learned his lesson quickly. Thankfully, out of costume, he was rarely recognized, so Kendall headed for the subway station and descended underground.

He caught a train and found a seat. The doors slid closed and the train began to move. Instantly, the weariness from being onstage and active for hours caught up with him. But he didn't dare close his eyes, not on the subway. He'd made that mistake once, and it had cost him the bag he'd been carrying. He didn't make eye contact with anyone, and at his stop, he jumped off and walked down the platform to the exit. He climbed the stairs and exited the station before walking down the familiar sidewalk to the west side midtown brownstone he called home. Kendall let himself into the building and climbed the stairs to his second-floor apartment.

"You're home," Johnny said as Kendall closed the door. They kissed in greeting, and Kendall dropped his bags on the floor. "How was it?"

"Everything was fine until the second act. Then it seemed to hit everyone that this was the last night. We did a good show, but I think some of the energy was just different. It's hard to explain, but things were off. Not that the audience knew, but we did." Kendall knew he should take care of his stuff, but he was tired and didn't have the energy. Johnny, however, glared at the bags more than once until he picked them up and carried them into the bedroom. "They can wait for now," Kendall said, hoping Johnny would come sit beside him and commiserate a few minutes.

"I'll just go ahead and do it," Johnny said.

Kendall heard him moving around. He should have known Johnny wouldn't settle until everything was just where he wanted it. The television was on, and Kendall began watching a program about the Ice Age or some crap like that, and soon his eyes closed. He felt Johnny sit down at one point, but he was too tired to move and made no effort to curl next to Johnny. The gesture probably wouldn't be welcomed anyway.

"Kendall, are you going to fall asleep?"

"Probably," Kendall muttered.

"Then go to bed," Johnny said, and Kendall cracked his eyes open. He did notice that Johnny didn't say "come to bed," or even offer to take him to bed, the way he used to. Kendall definitely noticed that, but he wasn't sure what to do about it. He stood up and shuffled into the bathroom. He made sure to clean up well, and brushed his teeth before leaving the bathroom. In the bedroom, he stripped down and got under the covers.

After a few minutes of listening to the muffled sound of the television, Kendall got up and opened the bedroom door. "Johnny, are you coming to bed?" He wanted to be held, to have someone be with him on a night like this. Something he'd worked on for months was over and he didn't want it to be. He was at loose ends and hurting a bit.

"Not for a while," Johnny said. Then the light and sound from the television ended as Johnny turned it off. Kendall sighed and returned to bed; the last sounds he heard before falling asleep came from the keyboard as Johnny typed at his computer.

Kendall woke a few hours later. Johnny was snoring softly next to him, and Kendall was a bit cold, so he snuggled up to his partner of almost a decade and closed his eyes again. The warmth, comfort, and contentment from Johnny's skin against his was just what he needed, but as he was about to fall asleep, Johnny began tossing and turning and then used his weight to roll Kendall back to his side of the bed. Johnny's warmth then disappeared as he went back to his side of the bed. "I'm cold," Kendall groused softly.

"Then get a blanket," Johnny told him, and within seconds the soft snoring began again. Kendall sighed, pushed back the covers, and got out of bed. He went to the small closet, got an extra blanket, and spread it on his half the bed, careful not to put it over Johnny or he'd be too warm. Kendall then got back into bed and closed his eyes. Johnny hadn't stirred, and Kendall, warm now, drifted back to sleep.

ANDREW GREY grew up in western Michigan with a father who loved to tell stories and a mother who loved to read them. Since then he has lived all over the country and traveled throughout the world. He has a master's degree from the University of Wisconsin-Milwaukee and now works full-time on his writing. Andrew's hobbies include collecting antiques, gardening, and leaving his dirty dishes anywhere but in the sink (particularly when writing). He considers himself blessed with an accepting family, fantastic friends, and the world's most supportive and loving husband. Andrew currently lives in beautiful historic Carlisle, Pennsylvania.

E-mail: andrewgrey@comcast.net
Website: www.andrewgreybooks.com

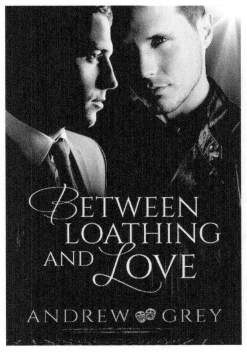

Theatrical agent Payton Gowan meets with former classmate—and prospective client—Beckett Huntington with every intention of brushing him off. Beckett not only made high school a living hell for Payton, but he was also responsible for dashing Payton's dreams of becoming a Broadway star.

Aspiring actor Beckett Huntington arrives in New York City on a wing and a prayer, struggling to land his first gig. He knows scoring Payton Gowan as an agent would be a great way to get his foot in the door, but with their history, getting the chance is going to be a tough sell.

Against Payton's better judgment, he agrees to give Beckett a chance, only to discover—to his amazement—that Beckett actually does have talent.

Payton signs Beckett but can't trust him—until Payton's best friend, Val, is attacked. When Beckett is there for him, Payton begins to see another side to his former bully. Amidst attempts by a jealous agent to sabotage Beckett's career and tear apart their blossoming love, Payton and Beckett must learn to let go of the past if they have any chance at playing out a future together.

www.dreamspinnerpress.com

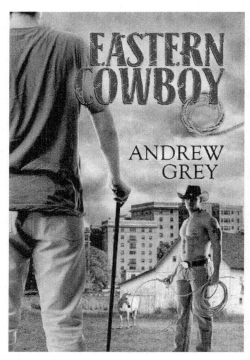

Brighton McKenzie inherited one of the last pieces of farmland in suburban Baltimore. It has been in his family since Maryland was a colony, though it has lain fallow for years. Selling it for development would be easy, but Brighton wants to honor his grandfather's wishes and work it again. Unfortunately, an accident left him relying on a cane, so he'll need help. Tanner Houghton used to work on a ranch in Montana until a vengeful ex got him fired because of his sexuality. He comes to Maryland at the invitation of his cousin and is thrilled to have a chance to get back to the kind of work he loves.

Brighton is instantly drawn to the intensely handsome and huge Tanner—he's everything Brighton likes in a man, though he holds back because Tanner is an employee, and because he can't understand why a man as virile as Tanner would be interested in him. But that isn't the worst of their problems. They have to face the machinations of Brighton's aunt, Tanner's ex suddenly wanting him back, and the need to find a way to make the farm financially viable before they lose Brighton's family legacy.

www.dreamspinnerpress.com

PATH NOT TAKEN

ANDREW GREY

On the train from Lancaster to Philadelphia, Trent runs into Brit, his first love and the first man to break his heart. They've both been through a lot in the years since they parted ways, and as they talk, the old connection tenuously strengthens. Trent finally works up the nerve to call Brit, and their rekindled friendship slowly grows into the possibility for more. But both men are shadowed by their pasts as they explore the path they didn't take the first time. If they can move beyond loss and painful memories, they might find their road leads to a second chance at happiness.

A story from the Dreamspinner Press 2015 Daily Dose package "Never Too Late."

www.dreamspinnerpress.com

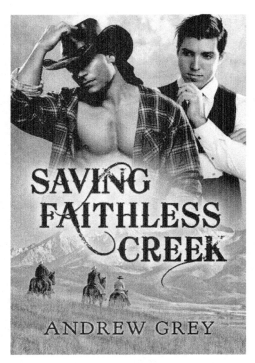

Blair Montague is sent to Newton, Montana, to purchase a ranch and some land for his father. It's a trip he doesn't want to make. But his father paid for his college education in exchange for Blair working for him in his casinos, so Blair has no choice. When he finds out he'll be dealing with Royal Masters, the man who bullied him in high school, he is shocked. Then Blair is surprised when he finds that Royal's time in the Marines has changed him to the point where Blair could be attracted to him… if he's willing to take that chance.

Royal's life hasn't been a bed of roses. He saw combat in the military that left him scarred, and not just on the outside. When he inherits his father's ranch, he discovers his father wasn't a good manager and the ranch is in trouble. The sale of land would put them back on good footing, but he is suspicious of Blair's father's motives, and with good reason. The attraction between them is hard for either to ignore, but it could all evaporate once the land deal is sealed.

www.dreamspinnerpress.com

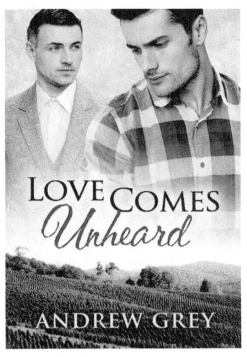

A Senses Series Story

Garrett Bowman is shocked that fate has brought him to a family who can sign. He's spent much of his life on the outside looking in, even within his biological family, and to be accepted and employed is more than he could have hoped for. With Connor, who's included him in his family, Garrett has found a true friend, but with the distant Brit Wilson Haskins, Garrett may have found something more. In no time, Garrett gets under Wilson's skin and finds his way into Wilson's heart, and over shared turbulent family histories, Wilson and Garrett form a strong bond.

Wilson's especially impressed with the way Garrett's so helpful to Janey, Connor and Dan's daughter, who is also deaf. When Wilson's past shows up in the form of his brother Reggie, bringing unscrupulous people to whom Reggie owes money, life begins to unravel. These thugs don't care how they get their money, what they have to do, or who they might hurt. Without the strength of love and the bonds of family and friends, Garrett and Wilson could pay the ultimate price.

www.dreamspinnerpress.com

Carlisle Cops: Book One

Officer Red Markham knows about the ugly side of life after a car accident left him scarred and his parents dead. His job policing the streets of Carlisle, PA, only adds to the ugliness, and lately, drug overdoses have been on the rise. One afternoon, Red is dispatched to the local Y for a drowning accident involving a child. Arriving on site, he finds the boy rescued by lifeguard Terry Baumgartner. Of course, Red isn't surprised when gorgeous Terry won't give him and his ugly mug the time of day.

Overhearing one of the officers comment about him being shallow opens Terry's eyes. Maybe he isn't as kindhearted as he always thought. His friend Julie suggests he help those less fortunate by delivering food to the elderly. On his route he meets outspoken Margie, a woman who says what's on her mind. Turns out, she's Officer Red's aunt.

Red and Terry's worlds collide as Red tries to track the source of the drugs and protect Terry from an ex-boyfriend who won't take no for an answer. Together they might discover a chance for more than they expected—if they can see beyond what's on the surface.

www.dreamspinnerpress.com

Carlisle Cops: Book Two

Carter Schunk is a dedicated police officer with a difficult past and a big heart. When he's called to a domestic disturbance, he finds a fatally injured woman, and a child, Alex, who is in desperate need of care. Child Services is called, and the last man on earth Carter wants to see walks through the door. Carter had a fling with Donald a year ago and found him as cold as ice since it ended.

 Donald (Ice) Ickle has had a hard life he shares with no one, and he's closed his heart to all. It's partly to keep himself from getting hurt and partly the way he deals with a job he's good at, because he does what needs to be done without getting emotionally involved. When he meets Carter again, he maintains his usual distance, but Carter gets under his skin, and against his better judgment, Donald lets Carter guilt him into taking Alex when there isn't other foster care available. Carter even offers to help care for the boy.

Donald has a past he doesn't want to discuss with anyone, least of all Carter, who has his own past he'd just as soon keep to himself. But it's Alex's secrets that could either pull them together or rip them apart—secrets the boy isn't able to tell them and yet could be the key to happiness for all of them.

www.dreamspinnerpress.com

Las Vegas Escorts: Book One

Hunter Wolf is a highly paid Las Vegas escort with a face and body that have men salivating and paying a great deal for him to fulfill their fantasies. He keeps his own fantasies to himself, not that they matter.

Grant is an elementary-school teacher who works miracles with his summer school students. He discovered his gift while in high school, tutoring Hunter, a fellow student. They meet again when Hunter rescues Grant in a club. Grant doesn't know Hunter is an escort or that they share similarly painful pasts involving family members' substance abuse.

After the meeting, Hunter invites Grant to one of the finest restaurants in Las Vegas. Hunter is charming, sexy, and gracious, and Grant is intrigued. With more in common than they realized, the two men decide to give a relationship a try. At first, Grant believes he can deal with Hunter's profession and accepts that Hunter will be faithful with his heart if not his body. Both men find their feelings run deeper than either imagined. For Grant, it's harder than he thought to accept Hunter's occupation, and Hunter's feelings for Grant now make work nearly impossible. But Hunter's choice of profession comes with a price, which could involve Grant's job and their hearts—a price that might be too high for either of them to pay.

www.dreamspinnerpress.com

Sequel to *The Price*
Las Vegas Escorts: Book Two

Ember is a drop-dead gorgeous Las Vegas escort. He notices Alejandro in some of the classes he teaches at his side business—a yoga studio. Then, color-blind Alejandro further captures Ember's attention when he's momentarily blinded by a quick change in light and needs Ember's help at a club. What Ember doesn't expect is the way Alejandro touches his heart.

Alejandro never intended to develop feelings for Ember. He's in Las Vegas for a year to sow some wild oats. But Alejandro quickly sees more in Ember when he sets out to make some of Alejandro's dreams come true—including a trip to the Grand Canyon and the beaches of LA. Alejandro's wild oats could turn into something memorable.

Ember knows keeping his escort job from Alejandro isn't the right thing to do, but he wants to be liked for who he is. Alejandro keeps his own secrets for the same reason. But Alejandro's family obligations, along with Ember's profession, could make it impossible for the two of them to stay together—unless they can figure out how to make the most of the gifts they've been given.

www.dreamspinnerpress.com

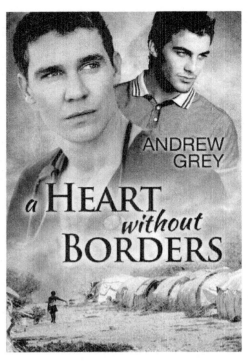

ANDREW
GREY

a HEART *without* BORDERS

Without Borders: Book One

Pediatrician Wes Gordon will do just about anything to escape his grief. When opportunity knocks, he signs on to work at a hospital in a tent camp in Haiti. One night while returning to his quarters, he comes across a gang of kids attempting to set fire to an underage rentboy and intervenes, taking the injured René under his wing. At the hospital, diplomat Anthony Crowley tells Wes that the kids involved in the attack are from prominent families and trying to hold them responsible will cause a firestorm.

In spite of the official position Anthony must take, Wes's compassion captures his attention. Anthony pursues him, and they grow closer during the stolen moments between Anthony's assignments, escaping earthquake destruction for glimpses of Caribbean paradise. When Wes realizes the only way to save René is to adopt him, Anthony is supportive, but time is running out: Wes must leave the country, and Anthony is called out on a dangerous secret mission. Now Wes must face adopting a boy from Haiti who has no papers without the support of the one person he's come to rely on most and may never see again.

www.dreamspinnerpress.com

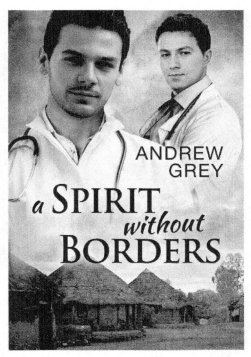

Sequel to *A Heart Without Borders*
Without Borders: Book Two

Dillon McDowell, an infectious disease specialist, jumps at the opportunity to work with Doctors Without Borders in Liberia. But when he arrives, things are very different than he expected, and he's out of his depth. Will Scarlet takes him under his wing and helps him adjust. A hint of normalcy comes when a group of local boys invite Dillon to play soccer.

Will's family rejected him for being gay, and he's closed off his heart. Even though meeting Dillon opens him to the possibility of love, he's wary. They come from different worlds, and Will plans to volunteer for another stint overseas. But Will realizes what Dillon means to him when Dillon becomes ill, and they can no longer deny their feelings.

When Dillon's soccer friends lose their parents and aunt to disease, Will and Dillon must work together to ensure that the boys aren't cast adrift in a society that's afraid they might be contagious. They must also decide if their feelings are real or just the result of proximity and hardship.

www.dreamspinnerpress.com

CPSIA information can be obtained at www.ICGtesting.com
Printed in the USA
BVOW06s1542061215

429498BV00010B/188/P